Dinabandhu Mitra

Nil Darpan

The indigo planting mirror - a drama

Dinabandhu Mitra

Nil Darpan
The indigo planting mirror - a drama

ISBN/EAN: 9783337382629

Printed in Europe, USA, Canada, Australia, Japan

Cover: Foto ©Andreas Hilbeck / pixelio.de

More available books at **www.hansebooks.com**

NIL DARPAN,

OR

THE INDIGO PLANTING MIRROR,

A Drama.

TRANSLATED FROM THE BENGALI

BY

A NATIVE.

―――――――

·

CALCUTTA:

C. H. MANUEL, CALCUTTA PRINTING AND PUBLISHING PRESS, No. 10,
WESTON'S LANE, COSSITOLLAH.

―――

1861.

INTRODUCTION.

THE original Bengali of this Drama—the NIL DARPAN, OR INDIGO PLANTING MIRROR—having excited considerable interest, a wish was expressed by various Europeans to see a translation of it. This has been made by a Native; both the original and translation are *bona fide* Native productions and depict the Indigo Planting System as viewed by Natives at large.

The Drama is the favourite mode with the Hindus for describing certain states of society, manners, customs. Since the days of Sir W. Jones, by scholars at Paris, St. Petersburgh, and London, the Sanskrit Drama has, in this point of view, been highly appreciated. The Bengali Drama imitates in this respect its Sanskrit parent. The evils of Kulin Brahminism, widow marriage prohibition, quackery, fanaticism, have been depicted by it with great effect.

Nor has the system of Indigo planting escaped notice : hence the origin of this work, the NIL DARPAN, which, though exhibiting no marvellous or very tragic scenes, yet, in simple homely language, gives the "annals of the poor ;" pleads the cause of those who are the feeble ; it describes a respectable ryot, a peasant proprietor, happy with his family in the enjoyment of his land till the Indigo System compelled him to take advances, to neglect his own land, to cultivate crops which beggared him, reducing him to the condition of a serf and a vagabond ; the effect of this on his home, children, and relatives are pointed out in language, plain but true ; it shows how arbitrary power debases the lord as well as the peasant ; reference is also made to the partiality of various Magistrates in favor of Planters and to the Act of last year penally enforcing Indigo contracts.

Attention has of late years been directed by Christian Philanthropists to the condition of the ryots of Bengal, their teachers, and the oppression which they suffer, and the conclusion arrived at is, that there is little prospect or possibility of ameliorating the mental, moral, or spiritual condition of the ryot without giving him security of landed-tenure. If the Bengal ryot is to be treated as a serf, or a mere squatter or day-labourer, the missionary, the school-master, even the Developer of the resources of India, will find their work like that of Sisyphus—vain and useless.

Statistics have proved that in France, Switzerland, Holland, Belgium, Sweden, Denmark, Saxony, the education of the peasant, along with the security of tenure he enjoys on his small farms, has encouraged industrious, temperate, virtuous, and cleanly habits, fostered a respect for property, increased social comforts, cherished a spirit of healthy and active independence, improved the cultivation of the land, lessened pauperism, and has rendered the people averse to revolution, and friends of order. Even Russia is carrying out a grand scheme of serf-emancipation in this spirit.

It is the earnest wish of the writer of these lines that harmony may be speedily established between the Planter and the Ryot, that mutual interests may bind the two classes together, and that the European may be in the Mofussil the protecting Ægis of the peasants, who may be able "to sit each man under his mango and tamarind tree, none daring to make him afraid."

THE AUTHOR'S PREFACE.

I PRESENT " The Indigo Planting Mirror " to the Indigo
Planters' hands; now, let every one of them, having observed his face, erase the freckle of the stain of selfishness
from his forehead, and, in its stead, place on it the sandal
powder of beneficence, then shall I think my labour successful, good fortune for the helpless class of ryots, and preser-
vation of England's honor. Oh, ye Indigo Planters! Your
malevolent conduct has brought a stain upon the English
Nation, which was so graced by the ever-memorable names of
Sydney, Howard, Hall, and other great men. Is your desire
for money so very powerful, that through the instigation
of that vain wealth, you are engaged in making holes like
rust in the long acquired and pure fame of the British
people? Abstain now from that unjust conduct through
which you are raising immense sums as your profits; and
then the poor people, with their families, will be able to spend
their days in ease. You are now-a-days purchasing things
worth a hundred rupees by expending only ten;—and you
well know what great trouble the ryots are suffering from that.
Still you are not willing to make that known, being entirely
given up to the acquisition of money. You say, that some
amongst you give donations to schools, and also medicine in time
of need—but the Planters' donations to schools are more odious
than the application of the shoe for the destruction of a milch
cow, and their grants of medicine are like unto mixing the in-
spissated milk in the cup of poison. If the application of a little
turpentine after being beat by Shamchand,* be forming a dis-

---

* *Shamchand* is an instrument made of leather, used by the Planters
for beating the ryots.

B

pensary, then it may be said that in every factory there is a dispensary. The Editors of two daily newspapers are filling their columns with your praises; and whatever other people may think, you never enjoy pleasure from it, since you know fully the reason of their so doing. What a surprising power of attraction silver has? The detestable Judas gave the great Preacher of the Christian religion, Jesus, into the hands of odious Pilate for the sake of thirty rupees; what wonder then, if the proprietors of two newspapers, becoming enslaved by the hope of gaining one thousand rupees, throw the poor helpless people of this land into the terrible grasp of your mouths. But *misery and happiness revolve like a wheel*, and that the sun of happiness is about to shed his light on the people of this country, is becoming very probable. The most kind-hearted Queen Victoria, the mother of the people, thinking it unadvisable to suckle her children through maid-servants, has now taken them on her own lap to nourish them. The most learned, intelligent, brave, and open-hearted Lord Canning is now the Governor-General of India; Mr. Grant, who always suffers in the sufferings of his people, and is happy when they are happy, who punishes the wicked and supports the good, has taken charge of the Lieutenant-Governorship, and other persons, as Messrs. Eden, Herschel, etc., who are all well-known for their love of truth, for their great experience and strict impartiality, are continually expanding themselves lotus-like on the surface of the lake of the Civil Service. Therefore, it is becoming fully evident that these great men will very soon take hold of the rod of justice in order to stop the sufferings which the ryots are enduring from the great giant *Rahu*, the Indigo Planter.

PERSONS OF THE DRAMA.

GOLUK CHUNDER BASU.

NOBIN MADHAB
BINDU MADHAB } *Sons of Goluk Chunder.*

SADHU CHURN—*A neighbouring Ryot.*

RAY CHURN—*Sadhu's brother.*

GOPI CHURN DAS—*The Dewan.*

J. J. WOOD
P. P. ROSE } *Indigo Planters.*

THE AMIN OR LAND MEASURER.

A KHALASI, *a Tent-pitcher.*

TAIDGIR—*Native Superintendent of Indigo Cultivation.*

Magistrate, Amla, Attorney, Deputy Inspector, Pundit, Keeper of the Gaol, Doctor, a Cow-keeper, a Native Doctor, Four Boys, a Latyal or Club-man, and a Herdsman.

WOMEN.

SABITRI—*Wife of Goluk Chunder.*

SOIRINDRI—*Wife of Nobin.*

SARALOTA—*Wife of Bindu Madhab.*

REBOTI—*Wife of Sadhu Churn.*

KHETROMANI—*Daughter of Sadhu.*

ADURI—*Maid-servant in Goluk Chunder's house.*

PODI MOYRANI—*A Sweetmeat Maker.*

FIRST ACT—FIRST SCENE.

GOLUK CHUNDER BASU *and* SADHU CHURN *sitting.*

Sadhu. Master I told you then we cannot live any more in this country. You did not hear me however. *A poor man's word bears fruit after the lapse of years.*

Goluk. O my child! Is it easy to leave one's country? My family has been here for seven generations. The lands which our fore-fathers rented have enabled us never to acknowledge ourselves servants of others. The rice which grows, provides food for the whole year, means of hospitality to guests, and also the expense of religious services; the mustard seed we get, supplies oil for the whole year, and, besides, we can sell it for about sixty or seventy rupees. Svaropur is not a place where people are in want.—It has rice, peas, oil, molasses from its fields, vegetables in the garden, and fish from the tanks;—whose heart is not torn when obliged to leave such a place? And who can do that easily?

Sadhu. Now it is no more a place of happiness : your garden is already gone, and your relatives are on the point of forsaking you. Ah! it is not yet three years since the Saheb took a lease of this place, and he has already ruined the whole village. We cannot bear to turn our eyes in the southern direction towards the house of the heads of the villages (Mandal). Oh! what was it once, and what is it now! Three years ago, about sixty men used to make a daily feast in the house; there were ten ploughs, and about forty or fifty oxen ; as to the court-yard, it was crowded like as at the horse races ; when they used to arrange the ricks of corn, it appeared, as it were, that the lotus had expanded itself on the surface of a lake bordered by sandal groves ; the granary was as large as a hill ; but last year the granary not being repaired, was on the point of

falling into the yard. Because he was not allowed to plant
Indigo in the rice-field, the wicked Saheb beat the *Majo* and
Sajo Babus most severely; and how very difficult was it to
get them out of his clutches; the ploughs and kine were sold,
and at that crisis the two Mandals left the village.

Goluk. Did not the eldest Mandal go to bring his brethren
back?

Sadhu. They said, we would rather · beg ' from door
to door than go to live there again. The eldest Mandal is
now left alone, and he has kept two ploughs, which are nearly
always engaged in the Indigo-fields. And even this person is making preparations for flying off. Oh, Sir! I tell
you also to throw aside this infatuated attachment (*maya*)
for your native place. Last time your rice went, and this
time, your honour will go.

Goluk. What honor remains to us now? The Planter
has prepared his places of cultivation round about the
tank, and will plant Indigo there this year. In that case, our
women will be entirely excluded from the tank. And also
the Saheb has said that if we do not cultivate our rice-fields
with Indigo, he will make Nobin Madhab to drink the
water of seven Factories (*i. e.* to be confined in them).

Sadhu. Has not the eldest Babu gone to the Factory?

Goluk. Has he gone of his own will? The pyeadah
(a servant) has carried him off there.

Sadhu. But your eldest Babu has very great courage.
On the day the Saheb said, " If you don't hear the Amin, and
don't plant the Indigo within the ground marked off, then shall
we throw your houses into the river Betraboti, and shall
make you eat your rice in the factory godown;" the
eldest Babu replied, " As long as we shall not get the price
for the fifty bigahs of land sown with Indigo last year, we
will not give one bigah this year for Indigo. What do we
care for our house? We shall even risk (pawn) our lives."

Goluk. What could he have done, without he said that? Just see, no anxiety would have remained in our family if the fifty bigahs of rice produce had been left with us. And if they give us the money for the Indigo, the greater part of our troubles will go away.

NOBIN MADHAB enters.

O my son, what has been done?

Nobin. Sir, *does the cobra shrink from biting the little child on the lap of its mother on account of the sorrow of the mother?* I flattered him much, but he understood nothing by that. He kept to his word, and said, give us sixty bigahs of land, secured by written documents, and take 50 Rupees, then we shall close the two years' account at once.

Goluk. Then, if we are to give sixty bigahs for the cultivation of the Indigo, we cannot engage in any other cultivation whatever. Then we shall die without rice crops.

Nobin. I said, " Saheb, as you engage all your men, our ploughs, and our kine, every thing, in the Indigo field, only give us every year through our food. We don't want hire." On which, he with a laugh said, " You surely don't eat Yaban's* rice."

Sadhu. Those whose only pay is a belly full of food are, I think, happier than we are.

Goluk. We have nearly abandoned all the ploughs; still we have to cultivate Indigo. We have no chance in a dispute with the Sahebs. They bind and beat us, it is for us to suffer. We are consequently obliged to work.

Nobin. I shall do as you order, Sir; but my design is for once to bring an action into Court.

---

* The Mahomedans and all other nations who are not Hindus, are called by that name.

ADURI *enters.*

Aduri. Our Mistress is making noise within ; the day is far advanced ; will you not go to bathe, and take your food. The boiled rice is very near become dry.

Sadhu. (*Standing up.*) Sir, decide something about this, or I shall die. If we give the labour of one-and-a-half of our ploughs for the cultivation of nine bigahs of Indigo-fields, our boiling pots of rice will go empty. Now, I am going away, Sir, farewell, out eldest Babu.

(Sadhu goes away.)

Goluk. We don't think that God will any more allow us to bathe and to take food in this land. Now, my son, go and bathe.

(All go away.)

FIRST ACT—SECOND SCENE.

The House of Sadhu Churn.

RAY CHURN *enters with his plough.*

Ray. (*Holding his plough.*) The stupid Amin is a tiger. The violence with which he came upon me ! Oh my God ! I thought that he was coming to devour me. That villain did not hear a single word and with force he marked off the ground. If they take five bigahs of land, what will my family eat. First, we will shed tears before them ; if they don't let us alone, as a matter of course, we shall leave the country.

KHETROMANI *enters.*

Is my brother come home ?

Khetra. Father is gone to the house of the Babu's and is coming very soon. Will you not go to call my aunt ? What were you talking about ?

Ray. I am talking of nothing. Now, bring me a little water, my stomach is on the point of bursting from thirst. I told my brother-in-law* so much, but he did not hear me.

SADHU *enters, and* KHETROMANI *goes away.*

Sadhu. Ray, why did you come so early ?

Ray. O my brother, the vile Amin has marked off the piece of ground in Sanpoltola. What shall we eat ; and how shall I pass the year ? Ah, our land was bright as the golden champah.† By the produce of only one corner of the field, we satisfied the mahajans. What shall we eat now, and what shall our children take ? This large family may die without food. Every morning two *recas* (nearly 5 ℔s) of rice are necessary. What shall we eat then ? Oh, my Ill-fortune ! Ill-fortune (burnt forehead) ! what has the Indigo of this white man done ?

Sadhu. We were living in the hope of cultivating those bigahs of land ; and now, if these are gone, then what use is there of remaining here any more. And the one or two bigahs which are become saltish, they yield no produce. Again, the ploughs are to remain in the Indigo-field ; and what can we do. Don't weep now ; to-morrow we shall sell off the ploughs and cows, leave this village, and go and live in the Zemindary of Babu Basanta.

KHETROMANI *and* REBOTI *enter with water.*

Now, drink the water, drink the water ; what do you fear ? He who has given life, will provide also food. Now, what did you say to the Amin ?

Ray. What can I say ? He began to mark off the ground, on which it seemed as if he began to *thrust burnt sticks*

---

* Here the word is used sarcastically ; and is taken to mean the brother of the wife.

† The name of a beautiful yellow flower.

C

into my breast, I entreated, holding him by his feet, and wanted to give him money ; but he heard nothing. He said, go to your eldest Babu ; go to your father. When I returned, I only punished him with saying, " I shall bring this before the Court."

(Seeing the Amin at a distance.)

Just see, that villain *(Shálá)* is coming; he has brought servants with him, and will take us to the Factory.

The AMIN *and the two Servants enter.*

Amin.   Bind the hands of this villain.

(Ray Churn is bound by the two Servants.)

Reboti.   Oh ! What is this ? Why do they bind him ? What ruin ! What ruin ! *(to Sadhu)* Why do you stand looking on ? Go to the house of the Babus, and call the eldest Babu here.

Amin.   *(To Sadhu.)* Where shalt thou go now ? You are also to go with me. To take advances is not the business of Ray. We shall have much to bear with if we are to make signature by cross marks. And because you know how to read and to write, therefore you must go and make the signatures in the Factory Account-book.

Sadhu.   Sir, do you call this giving advances for Indigo ; would it not be better to call it the *cramming down* Indigo ?* Oh ! my Ill-fortune, you are still with me. That very blow through fear of which I fled, I have to bear again. This land was as the Kingdom of Rama before Indigo was established ; but the ignorant fool is become a beggar, and famine has come upon the land.

Amin.   *(To himself, observing Khetromani.)* This young woman is not bad-looking; if our younger Saheb can get her, he will, with his whole heart, take her. But

---

* There is a play here on the words *Dádan* and *Gádan.*

while I was unable to succeed in getting a peshkar's (over-seer's) post by giving him my own sister, what can I expect from getting him this woman ; but still she is very beautiful ; I will try.

Reboti. Khetra, go into the room.

(Khetromani goes away.)

Amin. Now, Sadhu, if you want to come in a proper manner, come with me to the Factory.

(Going forward.)

Reboti. Oh Amin ! have you no wife nor children ? Have you kept only the plough and this beating *(márpit)* ? Did he not want to drink a little water ? By this time he ought to take a second meal, how can he then, without taking any food, go to the Saheb's house which is at such a distance. I ask for the Saheb's grace ; just let him have some food; and then take him away. Oh! he is so very much troubled for his wife and his children. Oh ! he is shedding tears, his face is be-come dry. What are you doing ? To what a burnt-up land am I come ? Destruction has come upon me both in life and money. Oh! Oh! Oh! I am gone both in life and money. *(Weeps.)*

Amin. Oh, stupid woman ! Now stop your grunting. If you want to give water, bring it soon ; else I shall take him away. *(Ray Churn drinks water ; exit all.)*

FIRST ACT—THIRD SCENE.

THE FACTORY OF BEGUNBARI. THE VERANDA OF THE LARGE BUNGALOW.

Enter J. J. WOOD and GOPI CHURN DAS, *the Dewan.*

Gopi. What fault have I done, my Lord ? You are observing me day by day. I begin to move about early in the morning, and return home at three o'Clock in the afternoon.

Again, immediately after taking dinner, I sit down to look over papers about Indigo advances ; and that takes my time to twelve and sometimes to one o'Clock in the night.

Wood. You, rascal, are very inexperienced. There are no advances made in Svaropur, Shamanagar, and Santighata villages. You will never learn without Shamchand, (the leather strap).

Gopi. My Lord I am your servant. It is through favour only that you have raised me from the *peshkári* business to the Dewani. You are my only Lord, you can either kill me or can cut me in pieces. Certain powerful enemies have arisen against this Factory ; and without their punishment, there is no cultivation of Indigo.

Wood. How can I punish without knowing them ? As for money, horses, latyals (club-men), I have a sufficiency ; can they not be punished by these ? The former Dewan made known to me about those enemies. You do not. I have scourged those wicked people, taken away their kine, and kept their wives in confinement, which is a very severe punishment for them. You are a very great fool ; you know nothing at all. The business of the Dewan is not that of the Kayt caste ; I shall drive you off, and give the business to a Keaot.

Gopi. My Lord, although I am by caste a Káystha, I do my work like a Keaot (a shoe-maker). The service which I have rendered in stopping the rice cultivation and making the Indigo to grow in the field of the Mollahs, and also to take *(lákhraj)* his rent-free lands of seven generations from Goluk Chunder Bose, and to take away the iron crow* from the Government ; the work I have done for these, I can dare say, can never be done by a Keaot (a shoemaker). It is my

---

* An instrument made use of for breaking down buildings.

ill-fortune only (evil forehead) that I don't get the least praise for doing so much.

Wood. That fool, Nobin Madhab, wants the whole account settled. I shall not give him a single cowrie. That fellow is very well versed in the affairs of the Court; but I shall see, how that braggart takes the advances from me.

Gopi. Sir, he is one of the principal enemies of this Factory. The burning down of Polasapore would never have been proved, had Nobin no concern in the matter. That fool himself prepared the draft of the petition; and it was through his advice and intrigues that the Attorney so turned the mind of the Judge. Again, it was through his intrigues that our former Dewan was confined for two years. I forbade him, saying, " Babu Nobin, don't act against our Saheb ; and, especially as he has not burnt your house." To which he replied, " I have enlisted myself in order to save the poor ryots. I shall think myself highly rewarded, if I can preserve one poor ryot from the tortures of the cruel Indigo Planters ; and throwing this Dewan into prison, I shall have compensation for my garden." That braggart is become like a Christian Missionary ; and I cannot say what preparations he is making this time.

Wood. You are afraid. Did I not tell you at first, you are very ignorant ? No work is to be done through you.

Gopi. Saheb, what signs of fear hast thou seen in me ? When I have entered on this Indigo profession, I have thrown off all fear, shame, and honor ; and the destroying of cows, of Brahmins, of women, and the burning down of houses are become my ornaments, and I now lie down in bed keeping the jail as my pillow (*thinking of it*).

Wood. I do not want words, but works.

SADHU RAY, *the* AMIN, *and the two Servants enter, making salams.*

Why are this wicked fool's hands bound with cords?

Gopi. My Lord, this Sadhu Churn is a head ryot ; but through the enticement of Nobin Bose he has been led to engage in the destruction of Indigo.

Sadhu. My Lord, I do nothing unjust against your Indigo, nor am I doing now, neither have I power to do any thing wrong ; willingly or unwillingly I have prepared the Indigo, and also I am ready to make it this time. But then, every thing has its probability and improbability ; if you want to make powder of eight inches' thickness to enter a pipe half-an-inch thick, will it not burst ? I am a poor ryot, keep only one-and-a-half ploughs, have only twenty bigahs of land for cultivation ; and now, if I am to give nine bigahs out of that for Indigo, that must occasion my death, but my Lord, what is that to you, it is only my death.

Gopi. The Saheb fears lest you keep him confined in the godown of your eldest Babu.

Sadhu. Now, Sir Dewanji, *what you say is striking a corpse* (useless labor). What mite am I that I shall imprison the Saheb, the mighty and glorious.

Gopi. Sadhu, now away with your high flown language ; it does not sound well on the tongue of a peasant ; it is like a sweeper's broom touching the body.

Wood. Now the rascal is become very wise.

Amin. That fool explains the laws and magistrate's orders to the common people, and thus raises confusion. His brother draws the ploughshare, and he uses the high word *pratápsháli* "glorious."

Gopi. The child of the preparer of cow-dung balls is become a Court Naeb (deputy). My Lord, the establishment of schools in villages has increased the violence of the ryots.

Wood. I shall write to our Indigo Planters' Association to make a petition to the Government for stopping the schools in villages ; we shall fight to secure stopping the schools.

Amin. That fool wants to bring the case into Court.

Wood. (*To Sadhu*) You are very wicked. You have twenty bigahs, of which, if you employ nine bigahs for Indigo, why can't you cultivate the other nine bigahs for rice.

Gopi. My Lord, the debt which is credited to him can be made use of for bringing the whole twenty bigahs within our own power.

Sadhu. (*To himself*) O oh! *the witness for the spirit-seller is the drunkard ?* (*Openly*) If the nine bigahs which are marked off for the cultivation of the Indigo were worked by the plough and kine of the Factory, then can I use the other nine bigahs for rice. The work which is to be done in the rice-field is only a fourth of that which is necessary in the Indigo-field, consequently if I am to remain engaged in these nine bigahs, the remaining eleven bigahs will be without cultivation.

Wood. You, dolt, are very wicked, you scoundrel *(háramjádá)* ; you must take the money in advance; you must cultivate the land ; you are a very scoundrel (*kicks him*). You shall leave off every thing when you meet with Shamchand (*takes Shamchand from the wall.*)

Sadhu. My Lord, *the hand is only blackened by killing a fly, i. e.,* your beating me only injures you. I am too mean. We—

Ray. (*Angrily*) O my brother, you had better stop ; let them take what they can ; our very stomach is on the point of falling down from hunger. The whole day is passed, we have not yet been able either to bathe or to take our food.

Amin. O rascal, where is your Court now? (*Twists his ears*).

Ray. (*With violent panting*). I now die! My mother! my mother!

Wood. Beat that "bloody nigger," (*beats with Shamchand, the leather strap*).

Enter NOBIN MADHAB.

Ray. O thou Babu! I am dying! Give me some water. I am just dead!

Nobin. Saheb they have not bathed, neither have they taken the least food. The members of their family have not yet washed their faces. If you thus destroy your ryots by flogging them, who will prepare your Indigo? This Sadhu Churn prepared the produce of about four bigahs last year with the greatest trouble possible; and if with such severe beatings you make such cruel advances to them, that is only your loss. For this day give them leave, and to-morrow I myself shall bring them with me, and do as thou do'st bid me.

Wood. Attend to your own business. What concern have you with another's affairs. Sadhu, give your opinion quickly, as it is my dinner time.

Sadhu. What is the use of waiting for my opinion? You have already marked off the four bigahs of the most productive land; and the Amin has, to-day, marked off the remaining part. The land is marked without my consent, the Indigo shall be prepared in the same way; and I also agree to prepare it without taking any advances.

Wood. Do you say my advances are all fictitious you cursed wretch, bastard and heretic, (*beats him*).

Nobin. (*Covers with his hand the back of Sadhu*). My Lord, this poor man has many to support in his family. Owing to the beating he has got, I think, he will be confined in bed for a month. Oh! What pains his family is suffering? Sir, you have also your family. Now, what sorrow would affect the mind of your wife if you were taken prisoner at your dinner-time?

Wood. Be silent thou fool, braggart, low fellow, cow-eater. Don't think that this Magistrate is like that one of Amaranagara, that you can, for every word, lay complaints before him, and imprison the men of the Factory. The Magistrate of

Indrabad is as death to you. You rascal, you must first give me a hand-note to state you have received the advance for sixty bigahs of land, or else I shall not let you go this day. I shall break your head with this Shamchand, you stupid. It is owing to your not taking advances, that I have not been able to force advances on ten other villages.

Nobin. (*With heavy sighs.*) O my Mother Earth! separate yourself that I may enter into you. ●In my life I never suffered such an insult. O, oh !

Gopi. Babu Nobin, better go home, no use of making fuss.

Nobin. Sadhu, call on God, He is the only support of the helpless.

(Nobin Madhab goes away.)

Wood. Thou slave of the slave. Take him to the Factory, Dewan, and give him the advance according to rule.

(Wood goes away.)

Gopi. Sadhu, come along to the Factory. Does the Saheb forget his words ?

Now *ashes have fallen on your ready-made rice;* the Yama* of Indigo has attacked you, and you have no safety.

FIRST ACT—FOURTH SCENE.
GOLUK CHUNDER BASU'S HALL.

Enter SOIRINDRI *preparing a hair-string.*

Soirindri. I never did prepare such a piece of hair-string. The youngest Bou† is the most fortunate, since whatever I do in her name proves successful. The hair-string I have made, is the thinnest possible. According to

---

* Yama is Death, the king of terror.

† This is a term which is applied to one's son's wife; but sometimes, though rarely, it means wife.

D

the hair, the hair-string is made. Oh! how beautiful the hair
is ; it is like unto that of the Goddess Kali. The face
is as the lotus, always smiling. People may say whatever they choose to one whom they do not like. I don't
attend to that. For my part, I feel pleasure when I see the
face of the youngest Bou. I consider the youngest Bou in
the same light, as I do Bipin. The youngest Bou loves me
as her own mother.

SARALOTA *enters with a braid in her hand.*

Saralota. My sister, just see whether I have been able to
make the under part of this braid ? Is it not made ?

Soirindri. (*Seeing the braid.*) Yes, now it is well made.
O ! my sister, this part is made somewhat bad ; the yellow
does not look well after the red colour.

Saralota. I wove it by observing your braid.

Soirindri. Is the yellow after the red in that ?

Saralota. No ; in that the green is after the red. But
because my green thread is finished, therefore I placed the
yellow after that.

Soirindri. You were not able, I see, to wait for the
market-day. I see, my sister, every thing is in haste with you.
As it is said, "*Hurry is in Brindabun ; but as soon as the
desire rises, there is no more waiting.*"*

Saralota. Oh ! What fault have I committed for that ?
Can that be got in the market ? At the last market-day, my
mother-in-law sent for it ; but that was not got.

Soirindri. When they write a letter this time to my
husband's brother, we shall send to ask for threads of various
colours.

Saralota. Sister, how many days are there still remaining
of this month.

---

* This is only a quotation, explaining, by an example, the eagerness of the
mind when the desire is once excited.

Soirindri. (*Laughingly.*) On the place where the pain
is, the hand touches. As soon as his* College closes, he
shall come home, therefore you are counting the days. Ah !
my sister, your mind's words are come out.

Saralota. I say truly, my sister ; I never meant that.

Soirindri. How very good-natured our Bindu Madhab is ?
His words are honey. When we hear his letters read, they
rain like drops of nectar. I never saw such love towards
one's brother as his ; and also his brother shows the greatest
affection for him. When he hears the name of Bindu Madhab,
his heart overflows with joy, and it becomes, as it were,
expanded. Also, as he is, so our Saralota is, (*pressing Saralota's cheek*) Saralota is *as honesty itself* (*Saralota*). Have
I not brought with me my huká ? I see, that as I
cannot remain without it for a moment, that is the first
thing which I have forgotten to bring along with me.

Enter ADURI.

Aduri, will you just go and bring me some ashes of
tobacco ?

Aduri. Where shall I now seek for it ?

Soirindri. It is stuck on the thatched roof of the cook-
room, on the right side of the steps leading into the room.

Aduri. Then, let me bring the ladder from the thresh-
ing floor ; else how can I reach to the roof ?

Saralota. Very well.

Soirindri. Why can she not understand our mother-in-
law's word ? Don't you understand what steps are, and what
Dain† signifies ?

Aduri. Why shall I become a Dain ; it is my fate. *As
soon as a poor woman becomes old and her teeth fall out*

---

* This pronoun "his" refers to the husband of Saralota.

† This is a Bengalli term signifying sometimes *right* and sometimes
a witch.

she is immediately called a Dain. I shall speak of this to
our mistress ; am I become so old as to be called a Dain ?

Soirindri. (*Rising up.*) Youngest Bou, sit down, I am
coming ; to-day we shall hear the Betal of Vidyeasagar.

(*Soirindri goes away.*)

Aduri. That Sagar allows marriage to the widows ; fie !
fie ! Are there not two parties to that ? I am of the Ajah's *
party.

Saralota. Aduri, did your husband love you well ?

Aduri. O young Haldarni, do not raise that word of sorrow now. Even up to this day, when his face comes before
my mind's eye, my heart, as it were, bursts with sorrow.
He loved me very much. And he even wanted to give me a
daughter-in-law. He even did not give me time to sleep.
Whenever I felt drowsy, he said, "O my love, are you
sleeping."

Saralota. Did you call him by his name ?

Aduri. Fie ! fie ! fie ! The husband is one's Lord. Is it
proper to call him by his name ?

Saralota. Then, how did you call him ?

Aduri. I used to say, "O ! do you hear me."

Enter SOIRINDRI *again.*

Soirindri. Who has irritated this fool again ?

Aduri. She was inquiring after my husband, therefore
I was speaking with her.

Soirindri. (*Laughing.*) I never saw a greater fool than
this our youngest Bou. While having so many subjects of
talk, still you are exciting Aduri in order to hear from her
about her husband.

---

* The word Rajah is here pronounced in an odd form ; and it has reference
to those rajahs who were against widow marriage. As the word is pronounced
by a woman of the lower class, it is spelt here incorrectly.

Enter REBOTI *and* KHETROMANI.

Welcome, my dear sister, I have been sending for you for these many days ; still I see, you don't get time to come.   O our youngest Bou, here take your Khetra ; here she is come. She was troubling me for these days, saying, My sister Khetra, of the Ghose family, is come from her father-in-law's house ; then, why is she not yet coming to our house ?

Reboti. Yes, such is your love towards us.   Khetra, bow down before your aunt.

(Khetrŏmani bows down.)

Soirindri. Remain with your husband for life ; wear vermillion even in your white hair ; let your iron circlet* continue for ever, and the next time you go to your father-in-law's house, take your new-born son with you.

Aduri. The young Haldarni speaks most fluently before me ; but this young girl bowed down before her ; and she spoke not a single word.

Soirindri. Oh ! what of that.   Aduri, just go and call our mother-in-law here.

(Aduri goes out.)

The fool knows not what she says.   For how many months is she† with child ?

Reboti. Did I yet express that ?   The bad turn of my fortune *(broken forehead)* is such, that I yet cannot say whether that is actually the case or not ?   It is because that you are very familiar with us, that I tell it you : at the end of this month she will be in her fourth month.

Saralota. Khetra, why did you cut off the curls of your hair ?

Khetro. The elder brother of my husband was much displeased at seeing the curls in my hair.   Our mistress said,

---

* The iron circlet worn by a woman on her left hand, is the mark or sign of the husband being alive.

† Referring to Khetromani.

that curls agree best with prostitutes and women of rich families. I was so much ashamed at hearing his words, that from that very day I cut off my curls.

Soirindri. Youngest Bou, the shades of evening are spreading about ; just go, my sister, and bring the clothes.

Enter ADURI *again.*

Saralota. (*Standing up.*) Aduri, come with me; let us go up, and bring down the clothes.

Aduri. Let young 'Haldar first come home, ha! ha! ha!
(*Ashamed, Saralota goes away.*)

Soirindri. (*With anger, yet laughing.*) Go thou unfortunate fool ; at every word, you joke. Where is my mother-in-law ?

Enters SABITRI.

Yes, she is come.

Sabitri. Ghose Bou, art thou come, and hast thou brought your daughter with you ? Yes, you have done well. Bipin was making noise, therefore, I sent him out and am come here.

Reboti. My mother, I bow down before you. Khetra, bow down before your grand-mother. (*Khetromani bows down.*)

Sabitri. Be happy, be the mother of seven sons. (*Coughing aside.*) My eldest Bou, just go into the room, I think my son is up. Oh! my son has no regular time for bathing, neither for taking food. My Nobin is become very weak by mere vain thoughts—(*aside,* " Aduri ") Oh! my daughter, go in soon, I think, he is asking for water.

Soirindri. (*Aside, to Aduri.*) Aduri, calling for you.

Aduri. Calling for me, but asking for you.

Soirindri. Thou burnt-faced. Sister Ghose meet me another day.

(*Exit Soirindri.*)

Reboti. O my mother, here is none else. Some great danger has fallen upon me, that Podi Moyrani came to our house yesterday.

Subitri. Rama! Rama! Rama! who allows that nasty fool to enter his house? What is left of her virtue? She has only to write her name in the public notices.

Reboti. My mother, but what shall I do? My house is not an enclosed one. When our males go to take dinner outside, the house is no more a house; but you may call it a mart. That strumpet says (I do shrink at the thought), she says, that the young Saheb is become, as it were, mad at seeing Khetromani; and wants to see her in the Factory.

Aduri. Fye! fye! fye! bad smell of the onion! Can we go to the Saheb. Fye! fye! bad smell of the onion! I shall never be out any more alone. I can bear every other thing, but the smell of the onion I can never bear. Fye! fye! bad smell of the onion!

Reboti. But, my mother, is not the virtue of the poor actual virtue? That fool* says, he will give money, give grants of lands for the cultivation of rice; and also give some employment to our son-in-law. Fie! fie! to money. Is virtue something to be sold? Has it any price? What can I say? That fool was an agent of the Saheb, or else I would have broken her mouth with one kick. My daughter is become thunder-struck from yesterday; and now and then, she is starting with fear.

Aduri. Oh, the Beard! When he speaks, it is like a he-goat twisting about its mouth. For my part, I would never be able to go there as long as he does not leave off his onions and beard. Fie! fie! fie! the bad smell of the onion.

Reboti. Mother, again that unfortunate fool says, if you

---

* Referring to Podi Moyrani (sweet-meat maker).

do not send her with me, I shall take her away by certain latyals

Sabitri. What more is the Burmese (Mug) power ? Can any one take away a woman from a house in the British Dominion ?

Reboti. O my Mother ! Every violence can be committed in the ryot's house. Taking away the women, they bring the men under their power. In giving advances for Indigo they can do this ; only they cannot commit this before one's eyes. Don't you know, my mother, the other day, because certain parties did not agree to sign a fictitious receift of advances, they broke down their house and took away by force the wife of one of the Babus.

Sabitri. What anarchy is this ! Did you inform Sadhu of this.

Reboti. No, my mother. He is already become mad on account of the Indigo ; again, if he hear this, will he keep quiet ? Through excessive anger he will rather smite his head with the axe.

Sabitri. Very well, I shall make this known to Sadhu, through my husband ; you need not say anything. What misfortune is this ! The Indigo Planters can do anything. Then why do I hear it generally said, that the Sahebs are strict in dispensing justice. Again, my son Bindu Madhab speaks much in praise of. them. Therefore I think that *these are not Sahebs ; no, they are the dregs, (Chandál) of Sahebs.*

Reboti. Respecting another word which Moyrani has said, I think the eldest Babu has not heard of it—that a new order has been proclaimed, by which the wicked Sahebs, by opening a communication with the Magistrate, can throw any one into prison for six months ; again, that they are making preparations for doing the same with the Babus.

Sabitri. (*Sighing deeply.*) If this be in the mind of God it will be.

Reboti. Many other things she said, my mother; but I was not able to understand her. Is it the fact, that there is no appeal when once a person is imprisoned?

Aduri. I think, the wretch has aggravated this imprisoning.

Sabitri. Aduri, be silent a little, my child.

Reboti. Moreover, the wife of the Indigo Planter, in order to make her husband's case strong *(pakka)*, has sent a letter to the Magistrate, since it is said that the Magistrate hears her words most attentively.

Aduri. I saw the lady; she has no shame at all. When the Magistrate of the Zillah (whose name occasions great terror) goes riding about through the village, the lady also rides on horseback, with him.—The Bou riding about on a horse! Because the aunt of Kesi once laughed before the elder brother of her husband, all people ridiculed her; while this was the Magistrate of the Zillah.

Sabitri. I see, wretched woman, thou wilt occasion some great misfortune one day. Now it is evening, Ghose Bou, better go home. There is Durga.

Reboti. Now, I go my mother. I shall buy some oil from the shop; then there will be light in the house.

(*Exit Reboti and Khetromani.*)

Sabitri. Can't you remain without speaking something at every word.

Enter SARALOTA *with clothes on her head.*

Aduri. Here, our washerwoman is come with her clothes.

Sabitri. Thou fool, why is she a washerwoman? *She is my Bou of gold, my Goddess of good Fortune (patting her back).* Is there no one in my family excepting you to

E

bring down the clothes ? Can't you, for one dunda* sit quiet
in one place ? Art thou born of such a mad woman ? How
did you tear off your cloth. I think you bruised yourself.
Ah, her body is, as it were, a red lotus ; and this one
bruise has made the blood to come out with violence.
Now, my daughter, I tell you, never move up and down the
steps in the dark, in such a mànner.

Enter SOIRINDRI.

Soirindri. Now, oyr young Bou, let us go to the ghât.

Sabitri. Now, my daughters, while the evening light con-
tinues, you two together go and wash yourselves.

(*Exit all.*)

SECOND ACT—FIRST SCENE.

The Godown of Begunbari Factory.

Torapa and four other Ryots sitting.

Torapa. Why do they not kill me at once ? I can never
show myself ungrateful. That eldest Babu, who has preserved my caste ; he through whose influence I am living here ;
he, who by preserving my plough and the cows, is preserving
my life,—shall I by giving false evidence throw the father of
that Babu into prison ? I can never do that ; I would rather
give my life.

First Ryot. *Before sticks there can be no words ;* the
stroke of Shamchand is a very terrible thrust. Have we
a film on our eyes ; did we not serve our eldest Babu ?
But, then, what can we do ? If we do not give evidence
they will never keep us as we are. Wood Saheb stood
upon my breast and blood began to fall drop by drop. *And
the feet of the horse were, as it were, the hoofs of the ox.*

---

* A dunda is equal to 24 English minutes.

Second Ryot. Thrusting in the nails ; don't you know the nails which are stuck under the shoes worn by the Sahebs ?

Torapa. *(Grinding his teeth with anger.)* Why do you speak of the nails ? My heart is bursting with having seen this blood. What do I say ? If I can once get him in the Vataramari field, with one slap I can raise him in the air ; and at once put a stop to all his "gad dams" and other words of chastisement.

Third Ryot. I am only a hireling, and keep men under me. When I heard about the plan which our master formed, I immediately refused to take any Indigo business on my hand, saying I shall never work for that. Why was I then confined in the godown ? I thought that serving under him at this time, I shall be able to make a good collection and shall be able to attend to my friend; but I am rotting here in this place for five days, and again I am to go to that Andarabad.

Second Ryot. I went to that Andarabad once or twice ; as also to that Factory of Bhabnapore, every one speaks good of the Saheb of that place ; that Saheb once sent me to the Court, then I saw many things pleasant in that place.

Torapa. Did he find any fault with you ? The Saheb of Bhabnapore never raises a false disturbance. *" By speaking the truth, we shall ride on horseback."* Had all Sahebs been of the same character with him, then none would have spoken ill of the Sahebs.

Second Ryot. My heart over-flows with joy.

Now his torturing is all put a stop to. In his godown there are now seven persons ; one of them a child. The vile man has filled his house also with kine and calves. Oh, what robbery is he carrying on !

Torapa. As soon as they get a Saheb who is a good man they want to destroy him. They are holding a meeting to drive off the Magistrate.

Second Ryot. I cannot understand whether they have found fault with the Magistrate of this or the other Zillah ?

Torapa. He did not go to dine in the Factory. They prepared a dinner for the Magistrate, in order to get him within their power, but the Magistrate *concealed himself like a stolen cow;* he did not go to dinner. He is a person of a good family. Why should he go to the Indigo Planters ? We have now understood, these Planters are the low people of Belata.*

First Ryot. Then how did the late Governor Saheb go about all the Indigo Factories, being feasted like a bride-groom just before the celebration of the marriage.† Did you not see that the Planter Sahebs brought him to this Factory well-adorned like a bride-groom ?

Second Ryot. I think he has some share in this Indigo Company.

Torapa. No ! can the Governor take a share in Indigo affairs ? He came to increase his fame. If God preserve our present Governor, then we shall be able to procure something for our sustenance ; and the great burden of Indigo shall no more hang on our shoulders.

Third Ryot. (*With fear.*) I die. If the ghost of this burden once attack a person, is it true that it does not quit him soon ? My wife said so.

Torapa. Why have you brought this my brother here ? For fear of the Sahebs, people are leaving the village ; and my uncle Bochoroddi has formed the following sentence :

" The man with eyes like those of the cat, is an ignorant fool ;
" So the Indigo of the Indigo Factory is an instrument of punishment."

---

* Belata means England.

† This refers to a certain practice in India of the Bride-groom going to the houses of relatives amid great feasting, before the celebration of the marriage.

Bochoroddi is very expert in forming such sentences.

Second Ryot. Did not you hear another sentence which was composed by Nitá Atai ?

" The Missionaries have destroyed the caste ;
" The Factory monkeys have destroyed the rice."

Torapa. Aola Nochen has composed " Destroyed the Caste," what is it ?

Second Ryot.

" The Missionaries have destroyed the caste :
" The Factory monkeys have destroyed the rice."

Fourth Ryot. Ha ! I do not know what is taking place in my house ; I am become the inhabitant of three villages at once. I came away to Svaropur, and through the advice of Bose, I threw away the advance which was offered me. When my young child was sick I came to Bose to get from him a little sugar-candy. Ah ! how very kind he was ; how agreeable and good-looking in countenance I found him ; and sitting as solemn as an elephant.

Torapa. How many bigahs have they given this year ?

Fourth Ryot. Last year I prepared ten bigahs ; but as to the price of that, they raised great confusion. This year again, they have given advances for fifteen bigahs ; and I am doing exactly as they are ordering me ; still, they leave not off insulting me.

First Ryot. I am laboring with my plough for these two years, and I have cultivated a little piece of ground. That piece of ground which I prepared this year, I kept for sesamum ; but one day, our young Saheb, riding on his horse, came to the place, and waiting there himself, took possession of the whole piece. How can the ryots live if this is to continue ?

Torapa This is only the intrigue of the wicked Amin. Does the Saheb know every thing about land ? This fool

goes about like a revengeful dog : when he sees any good piece
of land, he immediately gives notice of it to the Saheb. The
Saheb has no want of money, and he has no need for borrowing
money on credit. Then, why is it that the fool does so ; if he
have to cultivate Indigo, let him do so ; let him buy oxen ; let
him prepare ploughs ; if he cannot guide the plough himself,
let him keep men under him. What want have you of lands ?
If you can cultivate the whole village ; and we do not refuse
to give the village. In that case the land can overflow with
Indigo in two years. But he will not do it.

—*(Aside, ho ! ho ! ho ! má ! má !)* Gazi-Saheb ! Gazi-
Saheb ! Durga ! Durga !* call your Rama. Within this
there are ghosts. Be silent, be silent.

(Aside, Oh Indigo ! You came to this land for our utter
ruin. Ah ! I cannot any more suffer this torture. I cannot
say how many other Factories there are of this Concern.
Within this one month and-a-half, I have already drunk the
water of fourteen Factories ; and I do not know in what
Factory I am now ; and how can I know that, while I am
taken in the night from one Factory to another, with my
eyes entirely shut. Oh ! my mother where art thou now ?)

Third Ryot. Rama ! Rama ! Rama ! Kali ! Kali !
Durga ! Ganesha ! Ashra !

Torapa. Silence, silence.

(Aside, Ah ! I can make myself free from this hell, if I
take the advance for five bigahs of land. Oh ! my uncle, it
is now proper to take the advance. Now, I see no means
of giving the notice ; my life is on the point of leaving the
body. I have no more any power to speak. Oh my Mother,
where art thou now ? I have not seen thy holy feet for a
month-and-a-half.)

---

* These are all words used by Mahomedans in times of great alarm ; and
here it is used to express the fear of ghosts.

Third Ryot. I shall speak of this to my wife; did you hear now? Although these are become ghosts after death, still have they not been able to extricate themselves from the Indigo advances.

First Ryot. Art thou so very ignorant?

Torapa. A person of a good family; I have understood that by the words. My uncle Prana, can you once take me up on your shoulders, then I can ask him where his residence is?

First Ryot. Thou art a Musulman.

Torapa. Then, you had better rise on my shoulders and see —(*sits down*) rise up—(*sits on the shoulders*) take hold of the wall; bring your face before the window—(*seeing Gopi Churn at a distance*) come down, come down, my uncle, Gopi is coming (*first Ryot falls down*).

Enter GOPI CHURN *and* MR. ROSE *with his Ramkanta* in his hand.*

Third Ryot. Dewan, there is a ghost in this room. Now, it was crying aloud.

Gopi. If you don't say as I teach you, you must become a ghost of the very same kind. (*Aside, to Mr. Rose*) These persons have known about Mojumdar's confinement, we must no more keep him in this Factory. It was not proper to keep him in that room.

Rose. I shall hear of that afterwards. What ryot has refused; what rascal is so very wicked? (*Stamps his feet*).

Gopi. These are all well-prepared. This Musulman is very wicked; he says, I can never show myself ungrateful, (*nimak harámi*).

Torapa. (*Aside.*) O my father! How very terrible the stick is! Now I must agree with them; as to future considera-

---

* It is very like Shamchand.

tions I shall see what I can do afterwards. (*Openly*) Pardon me, Saheb! I, also, am become the same with you.

Planter. Be silent, thou child of the sow! This Ram-kant is very sweet. (*Strikes with Ramkant and also kicks him*).

Torapa. Oh! oh! my mother, I am now dead! My uncle Prana, give me a little water; I die for water. My father, father!

Rose. Shall not filth be discharged into your mouth? (*Strikes with his shoes*).

Torapa. Whatever thou shalt say, I shall do. Before God, I ask pardon of thee, my Lord.

Rose. Now the villain has left his wickedness. To-night all must be sent. Just write to the Attorney, that as long as the evidence is not given, not one of these shall be let out. The Agent shall go with them. (*To the Third Ryot*). Why art thou crying? (*Gives a kick*).

Third Ryot. Bou, where art thou? These are murdering me. O my mother! Bou! my mother! I am killed, I am killed. (*Falls upside down on the ground*).

Rose. Thou, stupid, art become (*bonra*) mad.

(*Exit Mr. Rose*).

Gopi. Now, Torapa, have you got your full of the onion and the shoe?

Torapa. Oh Dewanji, preserve me by giving a little water. I am on the point of death.

Gopi. The Indigo ware-house and the steam-engine room —these are places where the sweat shoots forth and water is drunk. Now, all of you, come with me, that you may at once drink water.

(*Exit all.*)

SECOND ACT—SECOND SCENE.

THE BED-ROOM OF BINDU MADHAB.

———

Saralota sitting with a letter in her hand.

Saralota. Now, my dear love with an honest tongue is not come, and an elephant, as it were, is treading on the lotus-like heart. I have become hopeless amid very great hope. In expectation of the coming of the Lord of my life, I was waiting with greater disquietude of mind than the swallow *(chátak)* does when waiting for the drops of rain at the approaching rainy season. The way in which I was counting the days exactly corresponded with what my sister said, that each day appeared, as it were, a year, *(deep sigh)*. The expectation as to the coming of my husband is now of no effect. The, course of his life itself will prove successful, if the great action in which he is now engaged, can prove so. Oh, Lord of my life ! We are born women, and cannot even go out to walk in the garden; we are unable to walk out in the city; can by no means form clubs for general good ; we have no Colleges nor Courts, nor Brahma Samajs of our own ; we have nothing of our own, to compose the mind, when it is once disturbed; and, moreover, we can never blame a woman when she feels any disquietude. O my Lord, we have only one to depend upon,—the husband is the object of the wife's thought, of her understanding, her study, her acquisition, her meeting, her society; in short, this jewel—the husband—is all to a virtuous woman. O thou letter ! thou art come from the hand of the dear object of my heart, I shall kiss thee, *(kisses it)* ; in thee is the name of my Lord ; I shall hold thee on my burnt heart, *(keeps it on her breast)*. Ah! how sweet are the words of my Lord; as often as I read it, my mind is more and more charmed *(reads)*.

My DEAR SARALA,—*In my letter I cannot express what anxiety my mind feels, to see your sweet face. O what inexpressible pleasure do I feel when I place your beautiful (moonlike) face on my breast! I thought that that moment of happiness is come; but pain immediately overtook pleasure. The College is closed, but a great misfortune has come upon me; through the grace of God, if I be not able to extricate myself from it, I shall never be able any more to show my face to thee. The Indigo Planters have secretly brought an accusation against my father in the Court; their main design being, in some way or other, to throw him into Jail. I have sent letters, one after another, to my brother, giving him this information; and I myself am remaining here with the greatest care possible. Never disturb yourself with vain thoughts ? The merciful Father must certainly make us successful. My dear, I have not forgotten the Benguli translation of " Shakespeare ;" it cannot be got now in the shops ; but one of my friends, Bonkima by name, has given me one copy. When I come home, I shall bring it with me. My dear, what a great source of pleasure is the acquisition of learning ! I am conversing with you, although at such a great distance, Ah ! what great happiness would my mind have enjoyed if my mother did not forbid you to send letters to me.*

" *I am, yours,*

" BINDU MADHAB."

As to myself—I have a full confidence as to that. If there be any fault in your character, then who should be an example of good conduct ? Because I am fickle ; cannot sit, for some time quietly in one place, my mother-in-law calls me the daughter of a mad woman. But, where is my fickleness now. In the place, where I have opened the letter

of my dear Lord, I have spent nearly a fourth part of the
day. The fickleness of the exterior part has now gone into
the heart. As, on the boiling of the rice, the froth rising up
makes the surface quiet, but the rice within is agitated ; so
am I now. I have not that smiling face now. A sweet
smile is the wife of happiness ; and so soon as happiness dies,
the sweet smile goes along with it. My Lord, when thou shalt
prove successful, every thing shall be preserved ; if I am to
see your face disquieted, all sides will be dark unto me. O
my restless mind, wilt thou be not quieted ? If you remain
unquiet, that can be suffered. As to your weeping, none can
see it, nor can hear it ; but my eyes ! you shall throw me into
shame, *(rubbing her eyes)*; if ye are not pacified, I shall not
be able to go out of doors.

Enter ADURI.

Aduri. What are you doing here ? The elder Haldarni* is
not able to go to the tank-side. All whom I see are of a
disturbed countenance.

Saralota. (*A deep sigh.*) Let us then go.

Aduri. I see you have not yet touched the oil. Your
hairs are yet dusty, and you have not yet left the letter.
Does our young Haldar write my name in the letter ?

Saralota. Has the Bara Takur (the eldest brother of
the husband) finished his bathing ?

Aduri. The eldest Haldar is gone to the village. A
law-suit is being carried on. Was that not written in your
letter ? Our master was weeping.

Saralota. (*Aside.*) Truly, my Lord ! Thou shalt not be
able to show thy face, if thou can'st not prove successful.
(*Openly*) Let us now rub ourselves with oil in the cook-room.

(*Exit both.*)

---

* Referring to Soirindri, the wife of Nobin Madhab.

SECOND ACT—THIRD SCENE.

A Road pointing Three Ways.

Enter Podi Moyrani.

Podi. It is the degenerate Amin who is ruining the country. Is it through my own choice that I am levelling the axe at my feet,* by giving the young woman to the Saheb? As to that preparation which Ray made, had it not been caught† by Sadhu, she would have been provided with food and clothing for life. Ah, it bursts my heart when I see the face of Khetromani. Have I no feelings of compassion, because I have made a paramour my companion? Whenever she sees me still, she comes to me, calling me Aunt! Aunt! Can the mother, with a firm heart, give such *a golden deer into the grasp of the tiger?* How detestable is this, that for the sake of money, I have given up my caste and my life; and also am obliged to touch the bed of a Buno (rude tribe). That libertine, the elder Saheb, has made it a practice to beat me whenever he finds me, and has also said, he will cut off my nose and ears ;—that vile man is come to an old age, can keep women in confinement, and can kick them ; such a vile man, I have not seen in the present day. Let me go to the black-mouthed Amin and tell him that shall not be effected by me. Have I any power to go out in the town? Whenever the nasty fellows of the neighbourhood see me, they follow me as the Phinga (a kind of bird) does the crow.

(*Aside, a song.*) Whenever I sit down to reap the rice in the field, his eyes immediately come before my sight.

---

* This expression " striking the axe on my feet" signifies ruining myself.

† That is, had the intrigue used by Ray not been detected, it would have proved very advantageous.

Enter a Cow-herd.

Cow-herd. *Saheb*, have not insects attacked thine Indigo-twigs ?

Podi. Let them attack thy mother and sister, thou degenerate fool. Leave off thy mother's breast, go to the house of Death ; go to Colmighata, to the grave.*

Cow-herd. I have also sent orders to prepare a pair of weeding knives.

Enter a Latyal or Club-man.

Oh ! the Latyal of the Indigo Factory.

The Cow-herd flies off swiftly.

Latyal. Thou, Oh lotus-faced, hast made the tooth-powder very dear.

Podi. (*Seeing the silver chain round the waist of the Latyal.*) Your chain is very grand.

Club-man. Don't you know, my dear, the clothing of the bailiff and the dress of the dancer ?

Podi. I wanted a black calf from you a long while ago, but yet you did not give it me. My brother, I shall not ask from thee any more.

Club-man. Dear lotus-faced, don't be angry with me. To-morrow, we shall go to plunder the place called Shama-nagara ; and if I can get a black calf, I shall immediately keep that in your cow-house. When I shall return with my fish, I shall pass by your house.

(*Exit the Club-man.*)

Podi. The Planter Sahebs do nothing but rob. If the ryots be loaded in a less degree with exactions they can preserve their lives ; and you† can get your Indigo. The Munshies of Shamanagara entreated most earnestly to get ten

---

* All these signify that let Death come upon thee.

† The word " you " refers to the Indigo Planters.

portions of land free. "*The Thief never hears the instructions of Religion.*" The wretched elder Saheb remained quiet, having burnt his wretched tongue.

Enter four Boys of a Native Patshala.

Four Boys. (*Keeping down their mats, and expressing great mirth with the clapping of their hands.*)

My dear Moyrani, where is your Indigo ?

My dear Moyrani, where is your Indigo ?

My dear Moyrahi, where is your Indigo ?

Podi. My child Kesoba, I am your aunt. ·Never use such words to me.   ℃

Four Boys. (*Dance together.*) My dear Moyrani ; where is your Indigo ?

Podi. My dear Ambika, I am your sister ; don't use me in this manner,

Four Boys. (*Dance round Podi.*)

My dear Moyrani, where is your Indigo ?

My dear Moyrani, where is your Indigo ?

My dear Moyrani, where is your Indigo ?

Enter NOBIN MADHAB.

Podi. What a shame is this, that I exposed my face to the elder Babu.

(*Exit Podi, covering herself with a veil.*)

Nobin. Wicked and profligate woman. (*To the children*) You are playing on the road still ; it is now too late, go home now.

(*Exit four boys.*)

Ah ! I can within five days establish a school for these boys, if only the tyranny of the Indigo be once stopped. The Inspector of this part of the country is a very good man. How very good a man becomes, if only learning be acquired. He is young ; but in his conversation he has the experience of years. He has a great desire that a school be

established in this country. I am also not unwilling
to give money for this purpose; the large Bungalow
which I have, can be a good place for a school; moreover,
what is more happy than to have the boys of one's own
country to read and write, and study in his own house, this is
the true success of wealth and of labour. Bindu Madhab
brought the Inspector with him, and it is his desire, that all
with one mind try to establish the school. But observing the
unfortunate state of the country, he was obliged to keep
his design to himself; how very mild, quiet, good-
natured, and wise is he become now! Wisdom in younger
years is as beautiful as the fruits in a small plant. In
reading of the sorrow which my brother has expressed in his
letter even the hard stone is melted and the heart of the
Indigo Planter would become soft. I cannot now rise up to
go home, I do not see any means; I was not able to
bring one of the five to my side, and I cannot find where
they are taken away.* I think Torapa will never speak
a lie. It shall be a great loss to us, if the other four give
evidence; especially as I was not able to make the least
preparation; and again the Magistrate is a great friend of
Mr. Wood.

*Enter a Ryot, two Peadas or Bailiffs of the Police, and
a Taidgir of the Indigo Factory.*

Ryot. My elder Babu, preserve my two children; there
is no one else to feed them. Last year, I gave eight carts'
load of Indigo, and I did not get a single pice for that, and
also I am bound, as with cords, for the remainder. Again,
they will take me to Andarabad.

Guard. The advance-money of the Indigo and the mark-
ing nut of the washer-man, as soon as they come in contact,

---

* This number, five, here referred to, are the persons whom he was trying
to bring on his side for the law-suit.

become mostly joined. You villain come ; you must first go to the Dewanji ; your elder Babu also shall come to this.

Ryot. Come, I don't fear this. I would rather have my body rot in the Jail than any more prepare the Indigo of that white man. My God ! my God ! none looks on the poor (*weeps*). My elder Babu, give my children food ; they brought me to the field ; and I was not able to see them once.

(Exit all, except Nobin Madhab.)

Nobin. What injustice ! These two children will die without food in the same way as the new-born young of the hare suffer when the hare is in the hand of the savage hunters.

Enter RAY CHURN.

Ray. Had not my brother caught hold of us, I would have put a stop to her breathing. I would have killed her ; then, at the utmost, I had been hanged within six months.* That villain !

Nobin. Ray Churn, where art thou going ?

Ray. Our mistress ordered me to call Putakur. The stupid Podi told me that the bailiff will bring the summons to-morrow.

(Exit Ray Churn.)

Nobin. Oh ! oh ! oh ! That which never took place in this family, has now come to pass. My father is very peaceful, honest, and of a sincere mind ; knows not what disputes and enmities are ; never goes out of the village ; trembles with fear at the name of Court affairs, and even shed tears when he read the letter. If he is to go to Indrabad, he will turn mad ; and if, to the jail, he will throw himself into the stream. Ah, such are the misfortunes that are to fall on him, while

---

* This expression " had been hanged for six months," is only used sarcastically.

I, his son, am living! My mother is not so much afraid as my father is; she does not lose hope at once; with a firm mind, she is now invoking God. My deer-eyed is become, as it were, the deer in my volcano*; she is become mad with fear and anxiety. Her father died in an Indigo Factory; and her fear, now, is lest the same happens to her husband. How many sides am I to keep quiet? Is it proper to fly off with the whole family; or, is it not right that to do good unto others is the highest virtue? I shall not turn aside hastily. I see, I am not able to do any good to Shamanagara; still, what work is there which is beyond the power of exertion? Let me see what I can do.

Enter two Pundits.

First P. My child, is the house of Goluk Chunder Bose in this quarter? I heard from my uncle, that person is very honest—the grandeur of the Bose family.

Nobin. *(Bowing before him.)* Sir, I am his eldest son.

First P. Yes! yes! very honest! To have such a son is not the result of a little virtue.

Second P. We had been invited by Babu Arabindu, of Sougandha. To-day, we remain in the house of Goluk Chunder; and shall do good unto you.

Nobin. This is my great fortune. Sirs, come by this way.

(Exit all.)

THIRD ACT—FIRST SCENE.

Before the Factory in Begunbari.

Enter Gopi Churn *and a Native Jailor.*

Gopi. As long as your share is not less, don't bring anything to my notice.

---

* That is, as the deer feels disquieted when exposed in a volcano, so is my mate troubled by the many anxieties in my mind.

G

Jailor. Can that filth be digested by one person eating the whole? I told him, if you eat, give a part to the Dewanji; but he says what power has your Dewan? He is not so much the son of a Keát, *(shoemaker caste)* that he shall direct the Saheb like unto one leading a monkey,

Gopi. Very well, now go; I shall show that Kaot (what a club) how strong he is.

(Exit Khálási.)

The fellow has got so much power through the authority of the younger Saheb. I shall also say it is a very easy thing for one to carry on his work, if his master bé the husband of his sister; the elder Saheb becomes very angry at this word. But the fellow is very angry with me; at every word, he shows me the Shamchand. That day he kicked me with his stockings on. These few days, I see that his temper is become somewhat mild towards me; since Goluk Bose is summoned, he has expressed a little kindness. A person is considered very expert by the Saheb, if he can bring about the ruin of many. "*One becomes a good Physician by the death of one hundred patients.*"

(Seeing Mr. Wood.)

Here he is coming; let me first soften his mind by giving him some information about the Boses.

Enter MR. WOOD.

Saheb, tears have now come out of the eyes of Nobin Bose. Never was he punished more severely. His garden is taken away from him; the small pieces of land he had are all included among the lands which are given to Gada, Poda *(low castes)*; his cultivation is nearly put a stop to; his magazines are all become empty, and he was sent into Court twice; in the midst of so many troubles, he still stood firm; but now he has fallen down.

Planter. That rascal was not able to do any thing in Shamanagara.

Gopi. Saheb, the Munshis came to him; but he told them, my mind is not at rest now, "my limbs are become powerless through weeping for my father, and I am, as it were, become mad." On observing the wretched condition of Nobin, about seven or eight ryots of Shamanagara have all given up, and all are doing exactly as your Honour is ordering them.

Planter. You are a very good Dewan, and you have formed a very good plan.

Gopi. I knew Goluk Bose to be a coward, and that if he were obliged to go to Court, he would turn mad. As Nobin has a great affection for his father, he will of course be punished; and it was for this reason that I gave the advice to make the old man the defendant. Also, the plan which your Honour formed was not the less good. Our Indigo cultivation has been newly made on the sides of his tank; thus laying the snake's eggs in his heart.

Planter. *With one stone two birds have been killed ;* ten bigahs of land are cultivated with Indigo, and also that fool is punished. He shed much tears, saying that if Indigo be planted near the tank we shall be obliged to leave our habitation; but I said, to cultivate Indigo in one's habitation is to the best advantage.

Gopi. And the fool brought an action in the Court, on hearing that reply.

Planter. That will be of no effect; that Magistrate is a very good man. If the case turn into a civil one it will never be concluded in less than five years. That Magistrate is a great friend of mine. Just see, by the new Act, the four rascals were thrown into prison only by making your evidence strong. *This Act is become the brother of the sword.*

Gopi. Saheb, in order that those four ryots might not suffer loss in their cultivation, Nobin Bose has given his own plough, kine, and harrow for the ploughing of their lands ; and he is trying his utmost that their families might not suffer great trouble.

Planter. When he is required to plough this land, for which advances are allowed, he says, my ploughs and kine are less in number. He is very wicked ; and now he is very well punished. Dewan, now you have done very well, and now I see work may be carried on by you, without loss.

Gopi. Saheb, it is your own favour. My desire is, that advances should be increased every year. But that cannot be done by me alone : some confident Amin and Khalasis are necessary. Can the Indigo cultivation be improved by those who, for the sake of two rupees, occasioned the loss of the produce of three bigahs of land ?

Planter. I have understood it, the rascally Amin occasioned this confusion.

Gopi. Saheb, the new habitation, and the taking of advances of Chunder Goladar are not allowed here. The Amin once, according to regular custom, threw one rupee on his ground as an advance. That person, in order to be allowed to return that rupee even shed tears and came along with the Amin as far as Ruthtollah, begging him earnestly to take it back. There he met with Nilkanta Babu, who has chosen the profession of an Attorney immediately after leaving the College.

Planter. I know that rascal ; he, it is, who writes every thing concerning me in the newspapers.

Gopi. Their papers can never stand before yours, can by no means bear a comparison ; and, moreover, they are as *the earthen bottles for cooling water compared to the jars of Dacca.* But, to bring the newspapers within your influence, great expense has been incurred. That takes place according to time ; as is said,

" According to circumstances, the friend becomes an enemy :
" The lame ass is sold at the price of the horse."

Planter. What did Nilkanta do ?

Gopi. He sharply rebuked the Amin ; and the Amin with no little shame brought back that one rupee, with two rupees more, from Goladar's house. Chunder Goladar would have been able very easily to supply the Indigo for three or four bigahs. Is this the work of a servant ? If I can conduct the Dewanny and the business of the Amin ; then this kind of ingratitude can be stopped.

Planter. Great wickedness this is ; evident ingratitude.

Gopi. Saheb, grant pardon for this bad conduct ; the Amin brought his own sister to our younger Saheb's room.

Planter. Yes ! Yes ! I know ; that rascal and Podi corrupted our young Saheb. I must give that wicked fool some instruction very soon. Send him to my sitting room.

(*Exit Mr. Wood.*)

Gopi. Just see, *in whose hand the monkey plays best. The Khait is one rogue, and the Crow another.*

" *Now have you fallen under the stroke of the Khait ; where even the grand-father of the sister's husband loses the game.*"

THIRD ACT—SECOND SCENE.

The Bed-room of Nobin Madhab.

NOBIN MADHAB *and* SOIRINDRI *sitting.*

Soirindri. Lord of my soul, what is preferable, whether the ornament or my father-in-law ? That, for which thou art wandering about day and night ; that, for which thou hast

left thy food and sleep; that, for which thou art shedding
tears incessantly; that, for which thy pleasant face has
been depressed; and that which has occasioned thy
head-ache; my dear Lord, can I not for that give away this
my trifling ornament.

Nobin. My dear, you can, with ease, give; but with what
face shall I take it? What great troubles the husband is to
undergo in order to dress his wife: he has to swim in the
rapid stream, to throw himself into the deep ocean, engage
in battles, to climb mountains, to live in the wilderness, and
to go before the mouth of the tiger. The husband adorns
his wife with so much trouble; am I so very foolish as to
take away the ornament from the very same wife. O my
lotus-eyed, wait a little. Let me see this day, and if,
finally I cannot procure it, then I shall take your ornaments
afterwards.

Soirindri. O my heart's love! We are very unfortunate
now; and who is there that shall give you on loan the sum
of Co.'s Rs. 500 at such a time. I am entreating you again,
take my ornaments and those of our youngest Bou, and try
to procure money from a banker. Observing your troubles
the lotus-like young Bou is become sad.

Nobin. Ah! my sweet-faced, the cruel words which you
used struck on my heart like arrows of fire. Our youngest
Bou, she is a girl; good clothes and beautiful ornaments are
objects of pleasure to her. What understanding has she
now? What does she know of family business. As our
young Bipin cries when his neck-lace is taken from him in
play, so our youngest Bou weeps when her ornaments
are taken away. Oh, oh! am I formed so mean-spirited
a man? Am I to be so cruel a robber? Shall I deceive a
young girl? This can never be, as long as life exists. The
worthless Indigo Planters even cannot commit such a crime.
My dear, never use such a word before me.

Soirindri. Beloved of my soul, that pain with which I told these words, is only known to me and the omniscient God. What doubt is there, that they are fiery arrows? They have burst my heart and burnt my tongue, and then having divided the lips, have entered your heart. It is with great pain that I told you to take the ornaments of the youngest Bou. Can there be any pleasure in the mind, after having observed this your insane wandering, this weeping of my father-in-law, the deep sighs of my mother-in-law, the sad face of the youngest Bou, the dejected countenance of relatives and friends, and the sorrowful mournings of the ryots? If by any means we can restore safety, then all shall be safe. My Lord, I do feel the same pain in giving the ornaments of our youngest Bou, as if I had to give those of Bipin; but if I give away the ornaments of Bipin, before giving those of the youngest Bou, that would prove an act of cruelty to her; since, she might think that my sister looks on me as a stranger. Can I give pain to her honest heart by doing this? Is this the work of the elder sister who is like a mother?

Nobin. My dear love! Your heart is very sincere. There is not a second to you in sincerity in the female race. Is this my family reduced to this state! What was I, and what am I now become! The sum of my profits was seven hundred Rupees. I had fifteen warehouses for corn, sixteen bigahs of garden land, twenty ploughs and fifty harrows. What great feasts had I at the time of the Puja; the house filled with men, feasting the Brahmins, gifts to the poor, the feasting of friends and relations, the musical entertainments of the Voishnabas, and also pleasant theatrical representations. I have expended such large sums, and even given as donations one hundred Rupees. Being so rich, now I am obliged to take away the ornaments of my wife, and the wife of my young brother. What affliction? God, thou didst give these, and thou hast taken them again. Then, what sorrow ?

Soirindri. My dear, when I see you weep, my life itself weeps *(tears in her eyes)*. Was there so much pain in my fate ; am I thus destined to see such distress in my Lord ? Do not prevent me any more. *(Takes out the amulet.)*

Nobin. My heast bursts when I see your tears *(rubbing the tears)*. Stop my dear, of the moon-like face, stop *(taking hold of her hands)*. Keep these ; one day more, let me see.

Soirindri. My dear, what further resource is left ? Do, as I tell you now. If it be so destined, there shall be many ornaments afterwards *(aside, sneezing)* ; true, true. Aduri is coming.

Enter ADURI *with two letters.*

Aduri. I can't say whence the letters came ; but my mistress told me to give them to you.

(Exit Aduri, after giving the letters.)

Nobin. It shall be known by these letters whether your ornaments are to be taken or not. *(Opens the first letter.)*

Soirindri. Read it aloud.

Nobin. *(Reads the letter.)*

" DEAR FRIEND,—*This is to make it known to you, that to give a sum of money to you at present is only to make a return of favours. My mother has taken leave of this world yesterday ; and the day of her first funeral obsequies is very near. This have I written yesterday. The tobacco is not yet sold.*

" I am, yours,

" GHONOSYAM MUKERJI."

What misfortune is this ! Is this my assistance on the funeral obsequies of the mother of the honorable Mukerji ?

Let me see what deadly weapon hast thou brought. *(Opens the letter.)*

Soirindri. My dear, it is very miserable to fall into despair after entertaining high hopes. Let the letter remain as it is.

Nobin. *(Reads the letter.)*

"HONORED SIR,—*I received your last letter, and was much pleased with reading of your good fortune. I have already collected the sum of three hundred Rupis, and shall take that along with me to you to-morrow. As to the remaining one hundred, I shall clear that on the coming month. The great benefit which you have bestowed on me, excites me to give some interest.*

"*I am, your most obdt. Servt.,*

"GOKUL KRISHNA PALITA."

Soirindri. I think God has turned his face towards us ; now, let me go, and give this information to our youngest Bou.

(Exit Soirindri.)

Nobin. *(Aside.)* My life is, as it were, the idol of sincerity ; it is a piece of a straw in a rapid stream. Let me take my father now to Indrabad, depending on this ; as to the future it shall be according to Fate. With me I have one hundred and fifty Rupis. As to the tobacco, if I had kept it for a month more, I would have sold that for the sum of five hundred Rupis ; but what can I do ? I am obliged to give it for three hundred and fifty Rupis, since I have to pay much for the Officers of the Court ; and also heavy expenses for going to and returning from the place. If on account of this false case, there be a delay, then am I certain that the destruction of this land is very near. What a brutal Act is passed ? But, what is the fault of the Act ; or of those who passed the Act ? What misery can the country suffer if those who are to carry out the Act, do it with impartiality ? Ah, by this Act how many persons are suffering in prison-houses without a fault ! It bursts the heart to see the miseries of their wives and children ; the pots for boiling rice on the hearths are remaining as they are ; the several kinds of grain in their yards are being dried up ; their kine in the rooms are all remaining bound in their places ; the cultivation of the fields is not fully carried out, the seeds are not sown, and the wild grass in the rice fields is not cut off. What further prospects are there in the present year ? All are crying aloud, with the exclamation, Where is my lord ? Where is my father ? Some Magistrates are dispensing justice with proper consideration ; in their hands this Act is not become the rod of death. Ah ! Had all Magistrates been as just as the Magistrate of Amaranagara is, then could the harrow fall on the ripe grain and the locusts destroy the fields ? Had that been the case, would I ever have been thrown into so many dangers ? O, thou Lieutenant-Governor ! had'st thou engaged men of the same good character as thou had'st enacted laws, then the country would never have been miserable. O, thou Governor of the land ! had'st thou made such a regulation, that every plaintiff, when his case is prov-ed false, shall be put in prison, then the jail of Amara-nagara would have been crowded with Indigo Planters ; and they would never have been so very powerful. Our Magis-trate is transferred, but our case is to continue here to the end ; and that will occasion our ruin.

(Enter Sabitri.)

Sabitri. If you are to give up all the ploughs, is it that even then you are to take the advance-money ? Sell all your ploughs and kine, and engage in trade ; we shall enjoy ourselves with the profits that shall accrue from that. We can no longer endure this.

Nobin. Mother, I, also, have the same desire. Only, I wait till Bindu is engaged in some service. If we leave off ploughing the land, ·it will be impossible for us to maintain the family ; and it is for this reason, that we have still, with so much trouble, kept these ploughs.

Sabitri. How shalt thou go with this headache ? Oh oh ! was such Indigo produced in this land ! (*Places her hand on Nobin's head*).

(*Enter Reboti.*)

Reboti. My mother ! Where shall I go ? What shall I do ? They have done what ! Why is it that through ill-fortune I brought her ? Having brought one of a strange caste, I am become unable to preserve propriety. My eldest Babu ! preserve me ; my life is on the point of bursting out. Bring me Khetromani ; bring me my *puppet of gold.*

Sabitri. These destroyers can do all things. Ye are taking by force the pieces of ground of men, their grain, their kine and calves. By the force of clubs, ye are cultivating Indigo, and the people are doing your work with cries and sobbings.

Reboti. My mother ! I am preparing the Indigo, taking only half the food. Those bigahs which they had marked, on them I worked. When Ray works, he weeps with deep sighs ; if he hear of this my work, he would become, as it were, insane.

Nobin. Where is Sadhu now ?

Reboti. He is sitting outside, and is weeping.

Nobin. To a woman of good family, *constancy in faithfulness to her husband is, as it were, the loadstone ;* and how very beautiful does she appear *(ramaniki ramaniyá)* when she is decorated with that ornament. Is a woman of a good family carried off, when the Bhima-like Svaropur of my father is still in existence ? At this very moment shall I go. I shall see what manner of injustice this is. *The Indigo frog can never sit on the white waterlily-like constancy of a woman.*

(*Exit Nobin Madhab.*)

Sabitri. Chastity is the store of gold which is given by Providence ; it is so valuable that it makes the beggar woman, a queen. If you can rescue this jewel before it is soiled, from the hands of the Indigo monkey, then shall I say that you have actually answered the purpose of my being your mother. Such injustice I never heard of. Now, Ghose Bou, let us go out-side.

THIRD ACT—THIRD SCENE.

MR. ROSE'S CHAMBER.   C

MR. ROSE *sitting. Enter* PODI MOYRANI & KHETROMANI.

Khetra. My aunt, don't speak of such things to me; I can give up my life, but my chastity never; cut me in pieces, burn me in the fire, throw me into the water, and bury me under ground ; but as to touching another man that can I never do. What will my husband think ?

Podi. Where is your husband now, and where are you ? This shall no one know. Within this night, I shall bring you back with me to your mother.

Khetra. Very well, the husband may not know it—but God above will know it, and I shall never be able to throw dust in his eyes. Like the fire of the brick-kiln it will still burn within my breast, and the more my husband shall love me for my constancy, the more my soul shall be tortured. Openly or secretly, I never can take a paramour.

Podi. My child, come, come to the Saheb. Whatever you have to say, say to him. To speak to me is like *crying in the wilderness.*

Planter Rose. To speak to me is *throwing pearls at the hog's feet.* Ha, ha, ha, we Indigo Planters, are become the companions of Death ; can our Factories remain, if we have pity? By nature, we are not bad ; our evil disposition has increased by Indigo cultivation. Before, we felt sorrow in beating one man ; now, we can beat ten persons with the Ramkant (leather strap), making them senseless ; and immediately after, we can, with great laughter, take our dinner or supper.

Torap. I will swim over the stream to my house, this night. What more shalt thou hear of my fate; I broke down the window of the Attorney's stable, and immediately ran off to the Zemindary of Babu Bosonto, and then in the night came to my wife and children. This Planter has stopped every thing ; has he left any means for men to live by ploughing? How very terrible are the thrusts of the Indigo? Again, the advice is given to serve for it. Now, Sir, where are your kicks with your shoes on, and your beating on the head? (*Thrusts him with his knees*).

Nobin. Torap, what is the use of beating him? We ought not to be cruel, because they are so ; I am going.

(Exit Nobin, with Khetromani.)

Torap. Do you want to show such ill-usage and bad conduct? Speak to your old father and carry on your business by mutual consent ; how long shall your force of hand continue? You shall not be able to do anything, when I shall fly. There is no abuse more horrid than to say, Die ! When your destiny shall decide, you shall have to enter the Factory of the Tomb. Just settle our eldest Babu's account of the last year ; and take what he consents to sow of Indigo in the present year. It is owing to you that they have fallen into a state of confusion. It is not merely to load one with advances, but cultivation is necessary. Good evening, our young Saheb. Now, I go. (*Throws him about, lying on his back, and flies off.*)

THIRD ACT—FOURTH SCENE.

THE HALL IN THE HOUSE OF GOLUK BOSE.

Enter SABITRI.

Sabitri. (*With a deep sigh.*) O thou cruel Magistrate! Why didst not thou also give me a summons? I would have gone to the zillah with my husband and my child; that would have been far better than remaining in this desert. Ah! my husband always remains in the house, never goes out to another village even on invitation. Is he destined to suffer so much?—The peadahs taking him away, and he himself to go to the jail. Bhagavati, my mother! was there so much in thy mind? Ah! he says, that he can never sleep, but in a room very long and broad; he eats only the boiled Atapa rice; * he takes the food prepared by no other hand but that of the eldest Bou. Ah! he brought out blood out of his breast by severe slaps; he made his eyes swollen by tears; and at the same time, he took his leave, he said this is my going to the side of the Ganges† (*weeps*). Nobin says, Mother call on Bhagavati. I must return home having gained my object and bring him home also. Ah! the face of my son, like unto that of gold, is blackened; what great troubles for the collection of money! Wandering about without rest, his brain is become like a whirl-pool. Lest I give away the ornaments of the Bous, my son encourages me, saying, My mother, what want of money? What large sum will be necessary for this case? How shall my child grieve, if my ornaments be given in mortgage for our suit on small portions of land! He says, as soon as I get a small sum of money, I shall immediately bring back the

---

* When the rice is cleansed from its husks by being placed in the sun, instead of being boiled, it is called the Atapa rice.

† That is, this is his last leave.

ornaments. My son has courage in his tongue and tears in his eyes. Ah ! he started with tears in his eyes. My dear Nobin, in this heat of the sun, went to Indrabad ; and I, a great sinner, remained confined in my room. Is this the life thy mother spends !

Enter SOIRINDRI.

Soirindri. Madam, it is now too late. Now bathe. It is our unfortunate destiny ; else, why shall such an occurrence come to pass ?

Sabitri. (*With tears.*) No, my daughter, as long as my Nobin does not return, I shall never give rice and water to my body. Who shall give food to my son ?

Soirindri. His brother has a lodging house there, and they have a Brahmin ; there will be no disturbance. You had better come and bathe.

Enter SARALOTA, *with a cup of oil.*

Young Bou, you had better rub the oil on her body, and make her bathe, and bring her to the cook-room. Let me go to prepare the place.

(*Exit Soirindri.*)

(*Saralota rubs the oil on her mother-in-law's body.*)

Sabitri. My parrot * is become silent ; my daughter has no more words in her mouth ; she is faded like a stale flower. Ah ! ah ! for how long have I not seen Bindu Madhab ? I am waiting in expectation that the College will be closed, and my son will come home. But this danger is come (*applying her hand on Saralota's chin*). Ah ! the mouth of my dear one is dry, I think you have not yet taken any food. While I have fallen into this danger,

---

* The word parrot here refers to Saralota. As the parrot is generally an object of fondness to persons, so Saralota was called a parrot, because she was much loved by her mother-in-law.

when shall I examine, whether any have taken their food or not. Let me bathe you, go and take some food. I am also going.

(Exit both.)

FOURTH ACT—FIRST SCENE.
THE CRIMINAL COURT OF INDRABAD.

Enter MR. WOOD, 'MR. ROSE, *the Magistrate, and an Officer, sitting.* GOLUK CHUNDER, NOBIN MADHAB, BINDU MADHAB, *the Attorneys of the Plaintiff and the Defendant, the Agent, Nazir, a Builiff, Servants, Ryots, &c., standing.*

Defendant's Attorney. May the prayer in this application be granted. *(Gives the application to the Sheristadar.)*

Magistrate. Very well; read it. *(Speaks with Mr. Wood, and laughs.)*

Sheristadar. *(To the Defendant's Attorney.)* You have written here what equals the length of the Ramayan. Can the petition be read without its being in abstract? *(Turns to another page of the application).*

Magistrate. *(Having spoken with Mr. Wood, and concealing his laughter).* Read clearly.

Sheristadar. In the absence of the defendant and his attorneys, the evidence is already taken from the witnesses of the plaintiff. We pray that the witnesses of the plaintiff be again called.

Plaintiff's Attorney. My Lord, it is true that attorneys are given up to lying, deceiving, and forgery; they easily forge and tell lies, and are incessantly engaged in immoral actions. They lead astray married women; and then they themselves enjoy their houses and every thing else. The Zemindars hate the attorneys; but for the effecting their

special purposes, they call them, and give them a seat on
their couch. My Lord, the very profession of the attorneys is a
cheating one. But the attorneys of the Indigo Planters can never
deceive. The Indigo Planters are Christians ; falsehood is ac-
counted a great sin in the Christian Religion. Stealing, licen-
tiousness, murder, and other actions of that nature are also
looked upon as hateful in that religion not taking evil actions
into consideration, even forming evil designs in the mind
dooms a man to burn in the fire of hell. The main aim of
the Christian Religion is to show kindness, to forgive, to be
mild, and to do good unto others ; so, it is by no means probable that the Indigo Planters, who follow such a true and
pure religion, ever give false evidence. My Lord, we do
serve such Indigo Planters ; we have reformed our character
according to theirs, and even, if we desire, we can, by no
means, teach the witness anything false ; since if the Sahebs,
the lovers of truth, find the least fault in their servants,
they punish them according to the rules of justice. The Amin
of the Factory, the witness of the defendant, is an example
of that. Because he deprived the ryot of his advances, the
kind Saheb drove him from his office ; and being angry on account of the cries of the poor ryot, he also beat him severely.

Wood the Planter.   (*To the Magistrate.*)   Extreme provocation ! Extreme provocation !

Plaintiff's Attorney.   My Lord, many questions were put
to my witnesses ; had they been witnesses who were prepared
ones (perjured) they would have been caught by those
very questions. The lawyers have said, " The Judge is as the
advocate of the defendant," consequently the questions to be
put by the defendant, are already asked by your Honour.
Therefore, there is no probability of any advantage to the defendant, if the witnesses be brought here again ; but on the
other hand, it will prove very disadvantageous to them.
Honored Sir, the witnesses are poor people who live by hold-

I

ing the plough. By the plough they maintain their wives
and children ; their fields become ruined if they do not remain there for the whole day ; so much so, that because it
proves a loss to them if they come home, their wives bring
boiled rice and refreshments bound in handkerchiefs to them
in the fields, and make them eat that. It proves an entire
loss to the ryots to come away from the fields' for one day ;
and at such a time, if they be brought to such a distant
part of the zillah by summons, then the labours of the whole
year will go for nothing. Honored Sir, Honored Sir, do as
you think just.   c

Magistrate. I don't see any reason for that (*as advised by
Mr. Wood*). There seems no necessity for that.

Defendant's Attorney. My Lord, the ryots of no village
take the advances of the Indigo Planters with their full
consent. The Indigo Planter, accompanied by the Amins and
servants, or his Dewan, goes on horse-back to the field, marks off
the best pieces of land, and orders the preparation of the Indigo.
Then the owner of the land brings the ryots to the Factory,
and having made known to them the particulars of the
matter, takes their signatures for the advances. The ryots,
taking the money in advance, come home with tears in
their eyes ; and the day on which any of them comes home
with the money, his house, becomes filled, as it were, with
the tears of persons weeping for the death of a relative or
friend. On the payment of the Indigo to the Indigo Planter,
even if the latter have something still to pay to the farmers
above the sum of the advances as the price of that
article, yet they keep it in their Account-books that the farmers have still something to pay. The ryots, when they have
once taken the advance, will suffer pain for not less than
seven generations. The sorrow which the ryots endure in the
preparation of the Indigo is known only to themselves and
the Great God, the Preserver of the poor. Whenever some sit

together, they converse about the advances and inform each other of their respective sums; and also try how to save themselves. They have no necessity for forming plans and mutually taking the advice of each other. Of themselves they are become as mad as the dog who received a blow on the head. The witnesses gave evidence that the ryots were willing to prepare Indigo ; but that the person who has engaged me had, by advice and intimidation, stopped their engaging in the preparation of Indigo. This is a very striking and an evident forgery. Honored Sir, once more bring them before the Bench, and your servant will by two questions disclose the falsity of their evidence. I do acknowledge, that Nobin Madhab Bose, the son of Goluk Chunder Bose, who engaged me, tried his utmost to extricate the helpless ryots from the hands of the giant-like Indigo Planters. I do acknowledge this. He also proved himself successful in stopping the tyranny of Mr. Wood ; which is known fully by the case which was brought here for the burning of the village of Polaspore. But Goluk Chunder Bose is of a very peaceful character ; he fears the Indigo Planters more than the tigers, never engages in any quarrels ; at no time injures another, and even is not courageous enough to save another from danger. My Saheb, that Goluk Chunder Bose is a man of a good character, is known to all persons in the zillah, and can be known even by enquiring of the Amlas of the Court.

Goluk. Honored Sir, the whole sum due for my Indigo of the last year was not paid; still only through fear of coming into Court, I consented to take the advance for sixty bigahs of land. My eldest son said, "Father, we have other ways of living ; the loss in Indigo for one year or two might stop feasts and religious ceremonies, but will not produce want of food. But those who entirely depend on their ploughs ; what means have they ? Losing this case if we be obliged again to engage in the Indigo cultivation, all will be obliged to do the

same afterwards." He said this is a wise man; and consequently I told him to make the Saheb, by entreaties and sup-
plications, to agree to fifty bigahs. The Saheb said nothing,
neither Yes nor No; and secretly made preparations to bring
me in my old age, to gaol. I know that the only way to get
happiness is to keep the Sahebs contented ; the country is the
Saheb's, the Judges are their brothers and friends; and is it
proper to do anything against them? Extricate me, and I
make this promise, that if I cannot prepare the Indigo
from want of ploughs and kine, I will annually give the
Saheb Co.'s Rs. 100 in the place of that. Am I a person to
tutor the ryots ? Do I meet them?

Defendant's Attorney. Honored Sir, of the four ryots who
came as witnesses, one is of the Tikiri caste ; he has no
knowledge of what a plough is ; he has no lands and no rents
to pay ; has no kine and no cow-house; and this can be best
known by proper examination. Kanai Torofdar is a ryot of
a different village ; and as to our Babu he has no acquaintance
with him. For these reasons we do pray that these men be
brought again. The legislators have said, before the decision,
the defendant ought to be supplied with all proper means.
Saheb, if this my prayer be granted, I shall have no more
reasons for complaint.

Plaintiff's Attorney. Saheb.

Magistrate. (*Writes a letter.*) Speak, speak ; I am not
writing from hearsay.

Plaintiff's Attorney. Saheb, if at this time, the ryots be
brought here they will suffer great loss ; else, I, also, would
have prayed for their being brought here again, since the
offences of the defendant which are already proved, may
receive stronger confirmation. Sir, the bad character of
Goluk Chunder Bose is known throughout the country;
he who benefits him, in return, receives injuries. The
Indigo Planters crossing the immeasurable ocean have come

to this land, and have brought out its secret wealth ; have done great benefit to the country, have increased the royal treasure, and have profited themselves. What place, besides the prison, can best befit a person who thus opposes the great actions of these noble men.

Magistrate. (*Writes the address.*) Chaprasi!

Chaprasi. Sir! (*Comes to the Saheb.*)

Magistrate. (*Advises with Mr. Wood.*) Give this to Mrs. Wood. Tell the Khansamah, the Saheb, who is come here, will not go to-day.

Sheristadar. Sir, what orders are to be written?

Magistrate. Let it remain within the *Nathi* or Court documents.

Sheristadar. (*Writes.*) It is ordered that it remains within the *Nathi* (*signed by the Magistrate*). Saheb, thou hast not yet made a signature on the orders to the reply of the defendant.

Magistrate. Read it.

Sheristadar. It is ordered, that the defendant is to give Co.'s Rs. 200, or two persons as security, and that the subpœnas be sent to the truthful witnesses. (*The Magistrate gives the signature*).

Magistrate. Bring the case of the robbery in Mirghan to the Court to-morrow.

(Exit Magistrate, Mr. Wood, Mr. Rose,
Chaprasi, and Bearers.)

Sheristadar. Nazir, take the security-bond from the defendant properly.

(Exit sheristadar, agent, the plaintiff's
attorney, the ryots.)

Nazir. (*To the Defendant's Attorney.*) How can we write now, while it is evening; moreover, I am somewhat busy now.

Defendant's Attorney. The name is great, but in property there is nothing (*speaks with the Nazir.*) This money they will give by selling the ornaments.

Nazir. I have no estates, have no trade nor lands for cultivation. This is my whole stock. It is for your sake only that I have agreed to take Rupees 100. Let us go to our lodging. Be careful that the Dewan does not hear this. Have not they got something as their own.

(Exit all.)

FOURTH ACT—SECOND SCENE.

INDRABAD, THE DWELLING of BINDU MADHAB.

NOBIN MADHAB, BINDU MADHAB, *and* SADHU *sitting.*

Nobin. I am now obliged to go home. My mother will die as soon as she hears of this. What more shall I do now for you? See that our father does not suffer great sorrow. I have now determined on leaving our habitation. I shall sell off everything, and send the money. Whoever wants any sum, I will give him that.

Bindu. The Darogah does not want money; only, for fear of the Magistrate, he does not allow the cooking Brahmin to be taken there.

Nobin. Give him money and also entreat him. Ah! His* body is old; he has been without food for three days! I explained to him, and entreated him greatly. He says, " Nobin, let three days pass and then shall I think, whether I shall take food or not ; within these three days, I shall not take any thing."

Bindu. I do not find any means, how I can be able to make my father take some boiled rice. The hand which he

---

* This pronoun refers to the father of Nobin.

has placed on his eyes from the time when the Magistrate, the slave of the Indigo Planters, ordered him to be kept in the prison, that hand he has not yet removed. The hand is filled with the tears; and the place where he was made to sit down at first, is still that where he now is. Being entirely silent, and remaining weak in body and without power to move, he is become like a dead pigeon in this cage-like prison. This day is the fourth, and to-day I must make him take food. You had better go home, and I shall send a letter every day.

Nobin. O God, what great sorrow art thou giving to our father ! If they do allow you, my dear Bindu, to remain day and night in the prison ; then can I quietly go to our house.

Sadhu. Let me steal, and you bring me before the Court as a thief. I will make the confession ; they will put me in prison ; then I will be best able to serve my master.

Nobin. O Sadhu ! Thou art the actual Sadhu (the honest man). Ah ! you are now very sorry on learning the deadly sorrow of Khetromani ; and the sooner I can take you home, the better.

Sadhu. (*Deep sigh.*) My eldest Babu ! Shall I see my daughter on my return. I have none other.

Bindu. If you make her take that draught which I gave you, she must be cured by that. The Doctor heard every particular of her disease, and has given that medicine.

Enter the Deputy Inspector.

D. Inspector. Bindu Babu, Mr. Commissioner has written very urgently about releasing your father.

Bindu. There is no doubt the Lieutenant-Governor will grant him release.

Nobin. After what time can the notice of the release come ?

Bindu. It will not be more than fifteen days.

D. Inspector. The Deputy Magistrate of Amaranagara gave an order of imprisonment for six months to a certain Mooktyar according to this law; but he had to remain for sixteen days in the gaol.

Nobin. Shall such a time ever come, that the Governor, becoming friendly, destroy the evil desires of the unfriendly Magistrate?

Bindu. There is a God, the Lord of the Universe; and he must do it. Sir, you had better start, for there is a long way to go.

(*Exit Nobin, Bindu, and Sadhu.*)

D. Inspector. Alas! The two brothers, burnt up by these anxieties, have, as it were, become dead, while living. The order of release from the Lieutenant-Governor will be as the restoration of life to them. Babu Nobin Chunder is of a brave spirit, does good to others, is very munificent, a great improver of learning, and also of a patriotic mind; but the mist of the cruel Indigo Planters withered all his good qualities in the bud.

Enter the Pundit of the College.

Welcome, Sir!

Pundit. My body is naturally somewhat of a warm nature. I cannot bear the sunshine. The heat of the sun makes me, as it were, mad in the months of March, April, and May. I had a very severe head-ache for a few days; and was not able to attend Bindu Madhab at all.

D. Inspector. The Vishnu Toila (a kind of oil) can do you some good. The oil is prepared for Babu Vishnu, and to-morrow I shall send some to your house.

Pundit. I am much obliged to you for that. A man of a healthy constitution becomes mad by teaching children; such am I.

D. Inspector. Why don't we see our elder Pundit any more?

Pundit. He is now trying some means to leave this doggish service. While his good son is making some acquisition of property, the family will be maintained like that of a King. It does not seem good for him now to go to and come from the College looking with his books under his arm like a bull bound to the cart. He is now of age.

Re-enter BINDU MADHAB.

Bindu. The Pundit is come.

Pundit. Did the sinful creature show so much injustice? You did not hear it ; at Christmas he spent ten days continually in that Factory. The ryot is to have justice from him ! *Can the Hindu celebrate his religious services before the Kazi* (the Mahomedan judge).

Bindu. The decree of Providence.

Pundit. Whom did you appoint as Muktyar ?

Bindu. Prandhan Mullik.

Pundit. Why did you appoint him as your Muktyar ? It would have been better if you had engaged some other person. " All Gods are equal. To make a separation from the wicked, the village becomes empty."*

Bindu. The Commissioner has made a report to the Government recommending the release of my father.

Pundit. *One is ashes and so is the other ;* as is the Magistrate such is the Commissioner.

Bindu. Sir, you know not the Commissioner ; and, therefore, you spoke thus of him. The Commissioner is very impartial, and is always desirous of the improvement of the natives.

Pundit. Whatever that be ; now if, through the blessing of God, your father be released, then all shall be well. In what condition is he in the gaol ?

---

* This is a proverb, signifying you cannot separate the tares from wheat.

Bindu. He is shedding tears day and night, and for the last three days has taken no food. Just now I shall go to the gaol, and shall make him happy by giving him this good news.

Enter a Chaprasi.

Art thou a chaprasi of the gaol?

Chaprasi. Sir, come quickly to the gaol. The Darogah has called you.

Bindu. Have you seen my father this day?

Chaprasi. Come, Sir. I cannot say anything.

Binda. Come, Sir (*to the Pundit*). I don't suppose all good. I go.

(*Exit Binda Madhab and Chaprasi.*)

Pundit. Yes; let us all go. I think some bad accident has taken place.

(*Exit both.*)

FOURTH ACT—THIRD SCENE.

The Prison-house of Indrabad.

The dead body of Goluk Chunder swinging, bound by his outer garment twisted like a rope; the Darogah of the Gaol and the Jamadar sitting.

Darogah. Who is gone to call Babu Bindu Madhab?

Jamadar. Manirodi is gone there. Till the Doctor comes, we cannot bring it down.

Darogah. Did not the Magistrate say, he will come here this day?

Jamadar. No, Sir, he has four days more to come. At Sachigunge on Saturday, they have a Champagne-party and ladies' dance. Mrs. Wood can never dance with any other, but our Saheb; and I saw that, when I was a bearer. Mrs.

Wood is very kind : through the influence of one letter, she got me the Jamadary of the Jail.

Darogah. Ah! The father of Babu Bindu Madhab expressed great sorrow at his not getting food. When Babu Bindu sees this, he will quit life.

Enter BINDU MADHAB.

All things are by the will of God.

Bindu. What is this! What is this! Ah! ah! My father is dead while bound above ground with a rope! I was coming to try some means for his release. What sorrow! (*places his own head on the breast of the dead body, then clasps the corpse, and weeps*). Oh father! Hast thou at once broken the ties of affection towards us? Shalt thou no more praise Bindu before other men for his English education? Calling Nobin Madhab by the name of " Bhima* of Svaropur ;" is that now put at an end? You have now made a treaty with Bipin (the son of Nobin) with whom you always had a quarrel, saying to the eldest Bou, " My mother, my mother." Ah! as in the case of a heron and its mate, with their young ones flying in the air, in search of food, if the heron be killed by a fowler, the mate with her young ones falls into great danger, so shall my mother be when she hears of your being put to death, while hung above ground by a rope.

Darogah. (*Bringing Babu Bindu aside by taking hold of his hands.*) Babu Bindu do not be so impatient now. Get the permission of the Doctor, and try to take the corpse soon to the Amritaghata.

Enter Deputy Inspector and the Pundit.

Bindu. Darogah, do not speak of anything to me. Whatever consultation you have to make, make that with the Pundit and the Deputy Inspector. Through sorrow, I

---

* Bhima or Brikadar was the second brother of Yudhistira and the second son of Pandu.

have lost the power of speech; let me take my father's feet once on my breast. (*Sits up, taking the feet of Goluk on his breast.*)

Pundit. (*To the Deputy Inspector.*) Let me take Bindu Madhab on my lap; you had better unloose the rope. It is never proper to keep such a godly body in this hell.

Darogah. It will be necessary to wait for a short time.

Pundit. Are you the chowkidar of hell, else why have you such a character?

Daroga. Sir, you are wise, you are reproaching me.

Enter the Doctor.   C

Doctor. Ho! Ho! Bindu Madhab! God's will. The Pundit is come. Bindu must not leave the College.

Pundit. It is not proper for Bindu to leave the College.

Bindu. As to our estates and possessions, we have lost every thing; at last, our father has left us beggars (*weeps*); how can studying be any more carried on?

Pundit. The Indigo Planters have taken away the all of Bindu Madhab and his family.

Doctor. I have heard of these Planters from the Missionaries and also I have seen them myself. Once as I was coming from a certain Planter's Factory at Matanagara, while I was sitting in a village, two ryots of the place were passing by the side of my palanquin; one of them had some milk with him, which I wanted to buy. Immediately, one whispered to the other, "The Indigo giant, the Indigo giant." Then having left the milk, they ran off. I asked another ryot, and he said, that these persons ran off for fear of being compelled to take advances for Indigo; and as I had taken the advance, what reason is there for going to his godown. I understood, he took me for a planter; I gave the milk into that ryot's hand, and went away from the place.

D. Inspector. A certain Missionary was passing through a village within the concern of Mr. Vally. As soon as the ryots saw him, they began to cry aloud, "The Indigo ghost is come out, the Indigo ghost is come out ;" and having left that path, flew into their own houses. But as the ryots found, by and by, the bounty, mildness, and forgiving temper of these gentlemen, they began to wonder ; and as much as the Missionaries showed heartfelt sorrow for the tortures which the poor people suffered from the Indigo Planters, so much the more they began to love them, and to have faith in them. Now the ryots say to each other, "All bamboos are of one tuft ; but of one is made the frame of the Goddess Durga, and of another the sweeper's basket."

Pundit. Let us take away the dead body.

Doctor. We must be sharp. You can bring it out.

(Bindu Madhab and the Deputy Inspector loosening the rope bring out the corpse.)

(Exit all.)

FIFTH ACT—FIRST SCENE.

BEFORE THE OFFICE OF THE BAGHUNBARI FACTORY.

Enter GOPINATH DAS *and a Herdsman.*

Gopi. How did you get so much information ?

Cowherd. We are their neighbours ; day and night, we go to their house. Whenever we are in want of any thing, either a little salt or a ladle of oil, we immediately go to them and bring it ; if the child cry, we bring a little molasses from them and give it ; we are getting our support for nearly seven generations from the Bose family ; and can't we get information about them ?

Gopi. Where was Bindu Madhab married ?

Cowherd. Oh, it is in a village to the west of Calcutta.

In which they wanted to have the Kaistas* wear the poita.
We cannot satisfy all the Brahmins now in existence in a great
feast, and still they wanted to increase the number. The father-
in-law of our young Babu is greatly respected. The Judge or
Magistrate when they come to him take off their hats.
Do such men give their daughters to men of these places?
Observing the improvements in learning made by our young
Babu, they did not care about the village belonging to ryots.
People say that the women in cities are showy, and
that there is no distinction between those who live within
the house and those who live in the bazar.† But we do
not at all find a young woman of a mild temper as the Bou
of the Bose family is. The mother of Goma goes to their
house every day, still, although she has been married for
nearly five years, she has never seen her face. We saw her
only on that day when she came here. We thought
that the Babus in the city keep company with the Europeans ; therefore they have brought their females into public
like English ladies.

Gopi. But the Bou is always engaged in attending on
her mother-in-law.

Cowherd. Dewanji, what shall I say ? The mother of
Goma says, I heard a report that, had not the youngest Bou
been in the house when the news of Nobin being bound by the
rope and thus killed came, the mistress of the family would
have died. We heard also that the women in the city treat
their husbands as sheep (slaves) and murder their parents by
not giving them any support ; but observing this Bou, I now
know that it is a mere report.

Gopi. I think, the mother of Babu Nobin Chunder also
loves her.

---

* The writer class among the Natives of this country

† Signifying the distinction between the women of a good and that of a
licentious character.

Cowherd. I don't see any one in the world whom she does not love. Ah! She is an Annapurnah* (full of rice). But have you kept the rice that she shall be full of it?† The vile Planters have swallowed up the old man, and they are now on the point of swallowing up the old woman.

Gopi. Thou braggart fool, if the Saheb hear this; he will bring out your new moon.‡

Cowherd. What can I do? Is it my desire to sit in the Factory and abuse the Sahebs?

Gopi. I am very sorry that I have destroyed this man of great honour by a false law-suit. I have also felt great pain on hearing of Nobin's severe head-ache and the miserable condition of his mother.

Cowherd. It is the cold attacking a frog.§ Dewanji, don't be angry with me, I am as a mad goat; shall I prepare the tobacco?

Gopi. This stupid fellow of Nanda's family is very senseless.

Cowherd. The Sahebs are doing all : *they themselves are blacksmiths and at the same time the cimeter ; where they make one to fall, there they themselves also fall.* If ruin come upon these Sahebs' Factories, then the people of the villages save themselves by bathing.‖ .

Gopi. You are very foolish. I don't want to hear any more? Go out, the Saheb will come very soon.

Cowherd. Now, I am going. You must attend to my milk bill, and also give me one rupi to-morrow. We shall go to bathe in the Ganges.

(Exit Cowherd.)

---

* This is one of the names of Durga, meaning the goddess of Plenty.

† Signifying, have you not taken away her whole possession ? Then, how can she show her pity by supporting the poor ?

‡ That is, he will make every thing dark to you, as at the time of the new moon. In short, he will kill you.

§ That is, nothing ; as the cold has no effect on the frog.

‖ That is, purify themselves by bathing.

Gopi. *I think the thunder-bolt will strike this head,* *which is aching.* No one will be able to stop the Saheb in sowing the Indigo seed on the sides of your tank. The Sahebs did something improper. These persons engaged themselves to sow Indigo on fifty bigahs of land, although they did not get the full price for the last year. Yet the Sahebs are not satisfied ; these disputes arose only for certain pieces of grounds ; and it would have been good for Nobin Bose to have given them these—*to keep the goddess Sitola* well-pleased is the best.* Nobin will bite once more even after his death. (*Seeing the Saheb at a distance*). Here the white-bodied man with a blue dress is coming. I think, I am to remain as a companion with the former Dewan for some days.

Enter MR. WOOD.

Wood. There will be a great quarrel at Matanagara : and all the latyals will be there. Let no one hear this ? For this place, make a collection of ten of the poda caste of (Surki) brickpowder makers or sellers. I, Mr. Rose, and you are to go there. The fool while he has taken his cacha† will not be able to increase the row greatly. He is sick ; then how can he go to bring assistance from the Darogah.

Gopi. The extreme weakness to which these are reduced, makes it unnecessary to bring any *surkiwallá* among the Hindus, for a person to die with a rope round his neck, especially within a prison is very disgraceful ; so he is greatly punished by this occurrence.

---

* Sitola is the goddess of the small-pox ; and the meaning of the above is that if that goddess be kept satisfied, the disease of the small-pox cannot come ; and if come, will pass away.

† This refers to Nobin Bose. The cacha signifies the piece of cloth kept by the sons on the death of their parents for one month, when the *pinda* or offering to the dead is made.

Wood. You do not understand this. The rascal is become very happy on the death of his father. He took the advances for a long time only through fear of his father ; now that fear is gone, and he will do as he likes. The rascal has given a bad name to my Factory, and I will imprison him to-morrow and keep him along with Mojumdar. If the Magistrate be of the same character with him of Amaranagara, the wicked people will be able to do every thing.

Gopi. With respect to what they planned about the case of Mojumdar, I cannot say how very terrible it would have been, had not Nobin Bose fallen into this great danger. I cannot say what they still will do? Moreover, as the Magistrate, who is coming, we have heard, is on the side of the ryots ; and when he comes to the villages, he brings along with him his tents.—Observing this, we may say, it might occasion great confusion, and also it is somewhat fearful.

Wood. You are always puzzling me with speaking of fear ; the Indigo Planters, in nothing whatever, have any fear. If you don't desire it, leave your business, thou great fool !

Gopi. Sir, fear comes on good grounds. When the former Dewan was put in prison, his son came to ask for the last six months' salary of his father. On which you told him to make an application. Then, on his making the application, you again said the salary cannot be given before the accounts are closed. Honored Sir, is this the judgment on a servant when he is put in prison ?

Wood. Did not I know this? Thou stupid, ungrateful creature ! What becomes of your salaries ? If you did not devour the price of the Indigo, would there be any deadly Commission ? Would the poor ryots have gone to the Missionaries with tears in their eyes ? You, rascal, have

L

destroyed every thing. If the Indigo lessen in quantity, I
shall sell your houses and indemnify myself; thou arrant
coward, hellish knave!

Gopi. Sir, *we are like butcher's dogs : we fill our bellies
with the intestines.* Had you, Sir, taken the Indigo from
the ryots in the very same way as the (Mahajans) factors take
the corn from their debtors, then the Indigo Factories would
never have suffered such disgrace; there would have been
no necessity for an overseer and the khalasis, and the people
would never have reproached me with saying " Cursed
Gopi! Cursed Gopi!"

Wood. Thou art blind, thou hast no eyes.

Enter an Umadar (an Apprentice).

I have seen with my own eyes (*applying his hand to his
own eyes*) the Mahajans go to the ricefield, and quarrel
with the ryots (their debtors). Ask this person.

Apprentice. Honored Sir, I can give many examples of
that. The ryots say, it is through the grace of the Indigo
Planters only that we are preserved from the hands of the
Mahajans.

Gopi. (*Aside, to the Apprentice.*) My child, it is vain
flattery. No employment is vacant now. (*To Mr. Wood*)
It is true that the Mahajans go to the rice-fields and dispute
with the ryots ; but if your Honor had been acquainted
with the mysterious intention of the Mahajans in going to
the fields and raising disputes, you would never have compared with the going of the Mahajans to the fields, the
punishment of the poor with Shamchand resembling the
tortures which Lakhman, the son of Sumitra, suffered by
the Sacti-sela,*—while they are without food.

---

* Lakhman was the brother of Rama. When they were gone to make
war with Ravana of Lunka, (Ceylon) in a certain battle Lakhman suffered
very much by the Sacti-sela (the name of a superior engine in a battle).

Wood. Very well, explain it to me. There must be some reason why these fools speak to us of every thing else; but of the Mahajans they don't say a single word.

Gopi. Honored Sir, these debtors, whatever sum of money they require for the whole year, they take from the Mahajans, and that quantity of rice which is necessary for them for that time, they also take from their creditors. At the end of the year, the debtors clear their debts either by selling the tobacco, sugar-cane, sesamum, and other things which they have, and then giving the sum collected to their creditors with the interest on the sum for the time; or by giving those very articles according to the market price: and of the corn which grows, they send to the Mahajans' houses, a part half-prepared. That which remains proves sufficient for the expenses of the family for three or four months. If through famine or any improper expenses of the debtors, there fall any arrears in their supplies, the remainder of the debt is carried into the new account-book. Then, by and by, the remainder is filled up. The Mahajans never bring an action against their debtors; consequently the falling into arrears appears to them, as it were, a present loss. I suppose the Mahajans for that reason, sometimes go to the fields, observe the preparation of the rice and also enquire whether the extent of land for which the debtors have asked the revenue from them, is all cultivated with grain. Some inexperienced persons, taking under false pretences a larger sum than is necessary, and thus being burdened with heavy debts, cause losses on the part of the Mahajans and also themselves suffer great trouble. The Mahajans go to the fields for stopping these, and not like " Indigo Giants" (*strikes his tongue*).* Sir, the stupid, shameless Mahajans speak thus.

---

* This is a sign of shame or fear.

Wood. I see, Saturn * has come upon you to your destruction ; else why art thou become so very inquisitive, and why so presumptuous, you stupid, incestuous brute ?

Gopi. Sir, we are made to swallow abuse, to submit to shoe-beating, and also we are the men to go to the Shrighur†‡ (the prison); the men should there be a dispensary or school in the Factory you get the credit ; should there be murders, we are the men. When I come to you for advice, you, Sir, become angry. That anxiety which I have felt for the law-suit of the Mojumdars, is only known to the Lord of all.

Wood. The fool is such, that whenever I tell him to do any action requiring courage, he brings to my ears the law-suit of the Mojumdar. I am saying always that thou art an ignorant fool ; why don't you become satisfied with sending Nobin Bose to the godown of Sochigunge.

Gopi. Thou, Sir, art the parent of this poor man ; it would be good, if for the benefit of thy poor servant, thou sendest him once to Nobin Bose to ask him about this case.

Wood. Stop, thou upstart of a son. Shall I go to meet a dog for you ? You coward son of a Kaista‡ (*throws him down with kicks*). Were you sent as a witness to the Commission, you would have ruined every thing, you diabolical niggar (*two kicks more*) ; with such a tongue you shall do your work like a Caot,§ you stupid Kaet. Were it not for your work on to-morrow, I would send you to the jail.

(Exit Mr. Wood and the Apprentice.)

Gopi. (*Rubbing his body all over and rising up*). A person becomes the Dewan of an Indigo Planter after being

---

* The planet Saturn is said to have a very bad influence. Whenever it comes upon one, the utter ruin of that person is thought very near.

† Ironically, the house of Prosperity.

‡ The Kaista is the caste of writers.

§ Caot is the name of a mean caste, and the word Kaet is only a common orm of expression for the term Kaista.

born a vulture* seven hundred times; else, how are numberless stockings digested ?† Oh! what kickings! Oh! the fool is, as it were, the wife of a student who is out of College.‡

(*Aside*) Dewan, Dewan.

Gopi. Your servant is present. Whose turn is it?

" In the sea of love are many waves."

(*Exit Gopi.*)

------◆------

FIFTH ACT—SECOND SCENE.

The Bedroom of Nobin Bose.

Aduri crying when preparing Nobin's bed.

Aduri. Ah! ha! ha! where shall I go? My heart is on the point of bursting. They have beaten him so severely that the pulse is moving very slowly; our mistress will die as soon as she sees this. When Nobin was taken by force to the Factory, they were tearing themselves and weeping under the shade of that tree; but when brought towards our house, they did not see that.

(*Aside.*) We shall take him into the house.

Aduri. Bring him into the house. None of them are here.

Enter Sadhu *and* Torapa *bearing the senseless Nobin on their shoulders.*

Sadhu. (*Making Nobin Madhab to lie on the bed.*) Madam, where art thou?

Aduri. They began to see, standing under the tree. When this person (*pointing to Torapa*) flew away with him, we thought he was taken to the Factory. They began to

---

* The vulture is taken for a detestable bird.

† Signifying, else how can he bear so many kickings?

‡ This is said only in reference to his dress.

tear themselves under the tree. I came to the house to call certain persons. Will our mistress remain alive when she sees this dead son? Do you stand here; let me call them here.

(Exit Aduri.)

Enter the Priest.

Priest. Oh God, hast thou killed such a man! Hast thou stopped the provision of so many men! We do not find any such symptom that our eldest Babu will sit up again.

Sadhu. God's will. He can give life to a dead man.

Priest. On the third day, Bindu Babu, according to the Shastras, celebrated the offering of the funeral cake (*pindadán*) on the banks of the Ganges; it is only through the entreaties of his mother that preparations are being made for the monthly ceremony *(shradh)*. It was determined that after the celebration of the ceremony, their dwelling place is to be removed; and I also heard that they will no more meet with that cruel Saheb; then why did he go there to-day?

Sadhu. Our eldest Babu has no fault, nor has he any want of judgment. Our madam and the eldest Bou forbad him many times. They said, " During the days we are to remain here, we will bathe with the water of the well, or Aduri will bring the water from the tank; we shall have no trouble." The eldest Babu said " With a present of 50 Rupis, I shall fall at the Saheb's feet, and thus stop the cultivation of the Indigo on the side of the tank, and shall speak nothing of the dispute in such a dangerous time." With this intention our eldest Babu took me and Torap with him, and going there with tears in his eyes, said to the Saheb, " Saheb, I bring you a present of 50 Rupis; only for this year, stop the cultivation of the Indigo in this place: and if this be not granted, take the money, and delay that business only till the time when the ceremony is to be performed." There is sin even in repeating the answer which the wretch gave, and the hairs of our body stood on an end. The rascal said, " Your father was hung in the jail of the Yabans* with thieves and robbers ; therefore keep your money for the sacrifice of many bulls which are necessary for his ceremony." Then placing his shoe on one of the eldest Babus knees, he said " This is the gift for your father's ceremony."

Priest. Narayan! Narayan.† (*Placing his hand on his ears*).

Sadhu. Instantly the eyes of the eldest Babu became red like blood, his whole body began to tremble, he bit his lips with his teeth and then remaining silent for a short time gave the Saheb a hard kick on the breast, so that he fell on the ground upside down like a bundle of *bena* (a certain grass). Kes Dali, who is now the jamadar of the Factory, and other ten surkiola immediately stood round him. The eldest Babu had once saved these from the hands of robbers ; so they felt a little ashamed to raise their hand against him. Mr. Wood gave a blow to the jamadar, took the stick out of his hand and smote with it the head of the eldest Babu. The head was cracked, and he fell down senseless on the ground ; I tried much, but was not able to go into that crowd. Torapa, was observing this from a distance : and as soon as the men stood round the eldest Babu, he with violence rushed into this crowd like an obstinate buffalo, took him up, and flew off.

Torapa. I was told " to stand at a distance, lest they take me away by force." The fools hate me very much ; do I hide myself when there is a tumult ? If I had gone a little before, I would have brought the Babu safe, and would have sacrificed two of those rascals in the Durgah of Borkat Bibi

---

* This term Yabans has reference to the Mahomedans, the Europeans.

† The name of Vishnu, God.

(the temple of Benediction). My whole body is shrunk on observing the head of the Babu ; then, when shall I kill these? Oh! oh! the eldest Babu saved me so many times, but I was not able to save him once. (*Beats his forehead and cries.*)

Priest. I see a wound from a weapon on his breast.

Sadhu. As soon as Torapa rushed into the crowd, the young Saheb struck the Babu with the sword. Torapa saved the Babu by placing, his hand in front of his own, which was cut, and there was the sign of a slight bruise on the Babu's breast.

Priest. (*Deeply thinking for some time, reads*).

" *Man knows this for certain, that understanding and goodness are necessary in the friend, the wife, and in servants.*" I do not see a single person in this large house ; but a person of a different caste and of another village, is weeping near the Babu. Ah ! the poor man is a day-laborer, and his very hand is cut off. Why is his face all daubed over with blood ?

Sadhu. When the young Saheb struck his hand with the sword, like an ichneumon making a noise when its tail is cut off, he in agony from the pain of his hand flew off after seizing with a bite the nose of the elder Saheb.

Torapa. That nose I have kept with me, and when the Babu will rise up alive again I will show him that (*shows the nose cut off*). Had the Babu been able to fly off himself, I would have taken his ears ; but I would not have killed him, as he is a creature of God.

Priest. Justice is still alive. The Gods were saved from the injustice of Ravana, when the nose of Surpanaka was cut off: shall not the people be saved from the tyranny of the Indigo Planters by the cutting off of the elder Saheb's nose ?

Torapa. Let me now hide myself; I shall fly off in the night. That fool will overturn the whole village on account of his nose.

(Exit Torapa bowing down twice on the earth near Nobin Madhab's bed.)

Sadhu. So very weak is our madam become by the death of her husband, that there is no doubt she will die, when she sees Babu Nobin in this condition. I applied so much water, rubbed my hand over the head, so long; but nothing is bringing him to his senses again. You, Sir, call him once.

Priest. Eldest Babu! Eldest Babu! Nobin Madhab! (*with tears in his eyes*) Guardian of ryots! Giver of food! moving his eyes now! Ah! The mother will die immediately. When she heard of his being bound with ropes above ground, she resolved not to take the rice of this sinful world for ten days. This is the fifth; this morning, Nobin Madhab taking hold of her shoulders shed much tears and said, " Mother, if thou dost not take food this day, then I shall never take the rice with the clarified butter; thus placing the sin of disobedience to the mother on my head; but shall remain without food." On which the mother kissing her son Nobin, said, " My son, I was a queen, now am I become the mother of a king. I would never have been sorry, had I once been able to place his* feet on my head at the time when he departed this life. Did such a virtuous person die an inauspicious death? It is for this reason that I am remaining without food. Ye are the children of this poor woman; looking on you and Bindu Madhab, I shall, this day, take for my food the orts of our reverend priest. Do not shed your tears before me."

(Aside, cries of sorrow.)

Coming.

---

* This pronoun " his" stands for Goluk Chunder, the father of Nobin Madhab.

Enter SABITRI, SOIRINDRI, SARALOTA, ADURI, REBOTI, *the Aunt of Nobin, and other women of the neighbour-hood.*

There is no fear, he is still alive.

Sabitri. *(Observing Nobin. on the point of death.)* Nobin Madhab! my son, my son, my son, where, where, where art thou! Oh! Alas!

(Falls senseless.)

Soirindri. *(With tears in her eyes.)* Oh young Bou! take hold of our mother-in-law; let me once see the Lord of my life, in the fulness of my heart. *(Sits near the mouth of Nobin.)*

Priest. *(To Soirindri.)* My daughter, thou art a great lover of thy husband, a woman of constancy; the frame of thy body was created in a good moment. For one who is so entirely devoted to her husband, and who has every thing good on her part, Fortune may give life to her husband again; he is moving his eyes, serve him without fear. Sadhu, remain here till our madam be in her senses.

(Exit Priest.)

Sadhu. Just see and place your hand on her nose. The body is become stiffer than that of a dead body.

Saralota. *(Speaking slowly to Reboti, after placing the hand on the nose.)* Her breathing is full, but the fire coming out of the head is so very intense that my throat, as it were, burns.

Sadhu. Has the Gomastah (head clerk) fallen into the hands of the Sahebs while he is gone to bring the physician? Let me go to the lodging-house of that physician.

(Exit Sadhu.)

Soirindri. Ah! Ah, my Lord! that mother for whose abstinence from food thou hast grieved so much; that mother, for whose weakness thou hadst served her feet ; that mother, who for some days was, by no means, able to sleep without placing thee in her lap, that very same dear mother is now lying senseless before thee, and thou art not seeing her once (*seeing Sabitri*). *As the cow losing her young one wanders about with loud cries, then being bit by a serpent falls down dead on the field ;* so the mother is lying senseless on the ground being grieved for her dear son. My Lord open thine eyes once more ; call thy maid-servant* once more with thy sweet voice and thus satisfy her ears once. . The sun of happiness has set at noon for me; what shall my Bipin do ? (*With tears in her eyes falls upon the breast of Nobin Madhab.*)

Saralota. Ye who an here take hold of our sister.

Soirindri. (Rising up). I became an orphan while very young ; it is for this death-like Indigo that my father was taken to the Factory, and he returned no more. That place became to him ʳthe residence of Yama (Death). My poor mother took me to the house of my maternal uncle, and there through grief for her husband, she bade adieu to the world. My uncles preserved me ; I remained like a flower accidently let fall from the hand of the gardener. My Lord took me up with love and increased my honour. I forgot the sorrow for my parents, and in the life of my husband my parents were, as it were, revived (*deep sigh*). All my griefs are rising up anew in my mind. Ah ! If I be deprived of that husband who keeps every thing under the shade of his protection, I shall again become the same helpless orphan.

Nobin's Aunt. (Raising her with the hands). What fear my daughter ? Why become so full of anxiety ? A letter is sent to Bindu Madhab to bring a doctor. He will be cured when the doctor comes. (*Falls down upon the ground.*)

---

* The term maid-servant here refers to Soirindri, the wife of Nobin Madhab.

Soirindri. My aunt-in-law, while I was a girl I made a celebration of a certain religious observance ; and placing my hands on the Alpana* (the white-washing prepared for the festival) prayed for these blessings : that my husband be like Rama, my mother-in-law like Kousalya, my father-in-law like Dasaratha, my brother-in-law like Lakshman. My aunt ! God gave me more than I prayed for. My husband is as Raghunath (Rama) brave and a provider of his dependants ; my mother-in-law is as Kousalya, having a sweet speech and an earnest love for her sons' wives ; my father-in-law is always happy in saying Badhumata, Badhumata,† and is the brightener of the ten sides.‡ Bindu Madhab, who surpasses the autumnal moon in purity, is dearer to me than was Lakshmandeva to Sita-devi. My aunt, all has taken place according to my desire ; only there is one in which I find some disagreement—I am still alive. Rama is making preparations for going to the forests, but there is no preparation for Sita's going with him§ Ah ! he was so much grieved on the abstinence of his father ; again, he took the cacha for the celebration of his funeral ceremony ; but before that was done he is preparing to go up to heaven (to die.) (*Looking on his face with a steady sight*) Ah ! his lips are dry. Oh ! my friends and companions, call my Bipin at once from the school ; I shall once more (*with weeping eyes*) through his hands pour a little water of the Ganges into his dry mouth. (*Places her mouth on that of his.*)

---

* It is a general custom in this country to apply the alpaua on the floor nearly in all religious observances.

† This term signifies the wife of one's son.

‡ This expression, " the brightener of the ten sides " signifies that he did good wherever he went. The ten sides are the north, south, east, west, north-east, north-west, south-east, south-west, the top, and the under sides.

§ The reference here is to the wanderings of Rama in the wilderness of the Deccan. The signification of the original is that while the husband Nobin is he on the point of death, there is no preparation for his wife to die with him.

All at once. Ah ! Ah !

Nobin's Aunt. (*Takes hold of her body and raises her.*) My daughter, do not speak such words now (*weeps*) ; if my sister were in her senses, her heart would have been burst.

Soirindri Oh ! mother, my desire is that my husband be happy in a future state in the same proportion as he had suffered misery in this. My Lord, I your bond-maid will pray to God for life ; thou wast most virtuous, the doer of great good to others and the supporter of the poor. The Great Lord of the Universe, who provides for the helpless, must give you a place. Ah ! take me, my Lord, with thee, that I may supply thee, with the flowers for the worship of God. "Ah ! what loss ! what ruin ! I see that Rama is going to the wilderness leaving his Sita alone. What shall I do ? Where shall I go ? and how shall I preserve my life ? Oh friend of the distressed, Oh Romanath ! Oh Great Wealth of the woman, supply me some means in this distress, and preserve me. I see that Nobin Madhab is now being burnt in the fire of Indigo. Oh, Lord of the distressed ! Where is my husband going now, making me unfortunate and without support," (*placing her hand on the breast of Nobin, and raising a deep sigh*). The husband now takes leave of his family, having placed all at the feet of God. Oh Lord, thou who art the sea of mercy, the supporter of the helpless, now give safety, now save !

Saralota. Sister, our mother-in-law has opened her eyes ; but is looking on me with a distorted countenance, (*weeping*). My sister, our mother-in-law never turned her face towards me with eyes so full of anger.

Soirindri. Ah ! ah ! our mother-in-law loves Saralota so much, that it is through insensibility only that with such an angry face she had thrown this champa on the burning

pot.* Oh my sister, do not weep now ; when our mother-in-
law becomes sensible she will again kiss you and with great
affection call you "the mad-woman's daughter." (*Sabitri
rises up and sits near Nobin ; and looking steadily on him,
with certain expressions of pleasure*).

Sabitri. There is no pain so excessive as the delivery of
a child, but that invaluable wealth which I have brought
forth made me forget all my sorrows on observing its face
(*weeping*). Ah ! if Madam Sorrow did not write a letter to
Yama (Death) and thus kill my husband, how very much
would he have been pleased on seeing this child. (*Clasps
with her hand*).

All at once. Ah ! ah ! she is become mad.

Sabitri. Nurse, put the child once more on my lap ; let
me pacify my burnt limbs. Let me once more kiss it in the
name of my husband. (*Kisses Nobin*).

Soirindri. Mother, I am your eldest Bou ; do you not see
me. Your dear Rama is senseless ; he is not able to speak now.

Sabitri. It would speak when it shall first get rice. Ah,
ah, had my husband been living what great joy ! How many
musical performances ! (*Weeps*).

Soirindri. It is misfortune upon misfortune ! Is my
mother-in-law mad now ?

Saralota. Take our mother-in-law from the bed, my sister;
let me take care of her.

Sabitri. Did you write such a letter, that there is no
musical performance on this day of joy ? (*Looking on all sides
and having risen from the bed by force, then going to
Saralota*) I do entreat thee, falling at thy feet, madam, to send
another letter to Yama, and bring back my husband for once.
Thou art the wife of a Saheb ; else, why shall I fall at thy feet ?

---

* That is, she had expressed so much anger against her ; or as the original, thrown her into the burning-pot of disgust and hatred. The Champa is
the name of a fragrant yellow flower.

Saralota. My mother-in-law, thou lovest me more than a mother, and such words from your mouth have given me more pain than that of death. (*Taking hold of the two hands of Sabitri*) Observing this your state, my mother, fire is, as it were, raining on my breast.

Sabitri. Thou strumpet, stupid woman, and a Yabana, why dost thou touch me on this eleventh day of the moon ?* (*Takes off her own hand*).

Saralota. On hearing such words from your mouth I cannot live (*lies down on the ground taking hold of her mother-in-law's feet*). My mother, I shall take leave of this world at your feet. (*Weeps*).

Sabitri. This is good, that the bad woman is dead. My husband is gone to heaven ; but thou shalt go to hell. (*Claps with her hand and laughs*).

Soirindri. (*Rising up*). Ah ! ah ! our Saralota is very good-natured. Now having heard harsh words from her mother-in-law, she is become exceedingly sorry ! (*To Sabitri*) Come to me, mother.

Sabitri. Nurse, hast thou left the child alone ? Let me go there. (*Goes to Nobin hastily, and sits near him*).

Reboti. (*To Sabitri*). Oh my mother ! Dost thou call that young Bou a bad woman, who you said was incomparable in the village ; and without whose taking food you never took food. My mother, you do not hear my words ; we were trained by you, you gave us much food.

Sabitri. Come on the Ata Couria† of the child, and I shall give you many sweetmeats.

Nobin's Aunt. My sister, Nobin will be alive again ; do not be mad.

---

* This day is kept sacred by the widows of this country.

† A certain ceremony performed on the eighth day after the birth for securing its good fortune.

Sabitri. How did you know this ? That name is known to
no one. My father-in-law said, when my daughter-in-law gets
a child, I shall give it (if male) the name "Nobin Madhab."
Now the child is born, I shall give it that name. My husband
always said, When shall the child be born, and I shall call him
by the name "Nobin Madhab" (*weeps*). If he had been
alive, he would have satisfied that desire on this day. (*Aside,
a sound*). There, the musicians are coming. (*Claps with her
hands*).

Soirindri. Bou, go into that room, the physician is
coming.

        Enter SADHU CHURN *and the Physician.*

                (*Exit Saralota, Reboti, and all the neigh-
                  bouring women ; and Soirindri, put-
                  ting a veil on her head, stands in
                  one side of the room.*)

Sadhu. Our madam has risen up.

Sabitri. (*Weeps.*) Is it because that my husband is not
here that you have left your drums at home.

Aduri. She has no understanding ; she is become
entirely insane. She called that dead elder Haldar
"My infant child," and chastised the young Haldar's wife,
calling her an European's wife. That young woman is weeping severely. Again, she is calling you musicians.

Sadhu. So great a misfortune has now come to pass !

Physician. (*Sitting near Nobin*). It is very probable
and also according to the Nidana* that while she is not
taking food for the death of her husband, and while she has
seen this miserable condition of her dearest son, she should
become thus. It is necessary to see her pulse one. Madam,
let me observe they pulse once. (*Stretching out his hand
towards her*).

---

* A treatise on the sciene of medicine.

Sabitri. Thou vile man must be a creature of the Factory, else why dost thou want to take hold of the hand of the woman of a good family ? (*rising up*). Nurse keep your eyes upon the child ; I go to take a little water. I shall give you a silk *sarhi.*

Physician. Ah ! the light of the understanding will not brighten again. I will send the Hima Sagara Toila (a medicinal oil) which is now necessary for her (*observing the pulse of Nobin*). His pulse is only very weak, but I do not find any other bad symptom. The doctors are ignorant in other matters, but in anatomical operations they are very expert The expense will be heavy, but it is of urgent necessity to call one in.

Sadhu. A letter has been sent to the young Babu to come along with a doctor.

Physician. That is very good.

Enter Four Relatives.

First. We never even dreamt that such an accident would come to pass. At noon-day, some were eating, some bathing, and some were going to lie down in their beds after dinner. I heard of it now.

Second. The stroke on the head appears fatal. What ill-fated accident ! There was no probability of a quarrel on this day ; or else, many of the ryots would have been present.

Sadhu. Two hundred ryots with clubs in their hands are crying aloud, "Strike off, Strike off," and are weeping with these words in their mouths, " Ah ! eldest Babu ! Ah eldest Babu !" I told them to go to their own houses, since if the Saheb get the least excuse, he will, on account of the of the pain in his nose, burn the whole village.

Physician. Now, wash the head and apply turpentine to it ; in the evening, I shall come again and try some other

means. To make noise in a sick person's room is to increase
his disease ; so, let there be no noise here.   -

> *(Exit the Physician, Sadhu Churn and the*
> *relatives in one way, and Aduri, the other ;*
> *Soirindri sits down).   The curtain falls.*

FIFTH ACT—THIRD SCENE.

The Room of Sadhu Churn.

On one side, Khetromani in great torment on her bed,
and Sadhu ; on the other side, Reboti, sitting.

Khetro.   Sweep over my bed ; mother, sweep over my bed !

Reboti.   My dear, dear daughter, why art thou doing so ?
I have swept on the bed ; there is nothing then on the coat
of shreds. I have placed another which your aunt gave.*

Khetro.   Thorns are pinching me, I die ! I die ! Oh ! turn
me to my father's side.

*Sadhu.   (Silently turning her to the other side. To him
self).*   This agony is the presage to death. *(Openly)*
Daughter, thou art the precious jewel of this poor man ; my
daughter, take a little food. I have brought some pome-
granates from Indrabad, and also the ornamented sarhi ;
but you did not at all express your pleasure when you saw
that.

Reboti.   How very extravagant are my daugther's desires !
She said once, give me a flower garland at the time of *Semon-
ton.*   What is that countenance now become ?   What shall I
do ?   Oh oh ! Oh oh ! *(Places her mouth on the mouth
of her daughter).*   Ah ! my Khetro of gold is become a
piece of charcoal. Where are the pupils of the eye ? See, see.

---

* Reboti says, My daughter, what is it that gives you so much pain ? The
bed is all over cleared, there is nothing that can trouble the body.

Sadhu. Khetromani! Khetromani! Open your eyes fully my daughter.

Khetro. My mother! my father! Ah, it is an axe! (*Turns on the other side*).*

Reboti. Let me take her on my lap; she will remain quiet there. (*Comes to take her on her lap*).

Sadhu. Do not take her up; she will faint.

Reboti. Am I so very unfortunate! Ah! Ah! My Harana is as Kartika on his peacock.† How can I forget him? Dear me! my Siva!

Sadhu. Raychurn is gone a long time ago; he is not yet come.

Reboti. Our eldest Babu preserved her from the grasp of the tiger. The young Saheb killed my daughter, and the elder one killed the eldest Babu. Ah! Ah! there is no one to preserve the poor.

Sadhu. What virtuous actions have I done, that I shall see the face of my grand-child?

Khetro. My body is cut off—a cracked Tangrah (a fish) Ah! ah!

Reboti. I think the ninth of the moon is closed;‡ my image of gold is to go to the water, and what means shall I have? Who shall call me mother! mother! Did you bring her for this purpose. (*Taking hold of Sadhu's neck, weeps*).

Sadhu. Be silent, don't weep now; she will faint.

---

* These are words which are expressed through great grief.

† Kartika is taken to be the most lovely in appearance among the gods —the symbol of male beauty. He is the son of Siva and Doorgah.

‡ Here, the reference is to the last of the three days in which the goddess Doorgah is worshipped; and the last day is taken to be one of great pain, because on that day she is to take her departure from her parents to go to her husband Siva.

Enter RAYCHURN *and the Physician.*

Physician. How is she now? Did you give her that medicine?

Sadhu. The medicine did not act, and whatever went down immediately came up by a vomit. See her pulse once more now; I think, it is a sign of her end.

Reboti. She is crying out, thorns, thorns. I have prepared her bed so thickly,* still she is tossing about. Now save her by a good medicine. Dear Sir, this relative is very dear unto me.

Sadhu. We don't see any sign of the pulse.

Physician. *(Taking hold of the hand).* In this state, it is good for the pulse to be weak. " Weakness makes the pulse strong ; to have a strong pulse is fatal."

Sadhu. At this time, it is the same thing either to apply or not to apply the medicine. The parents have hope to the very end ; therefore, see, if there be any means.

Physician. The water with which the Atapa (dried rice) is washed, is now necessary. The application of the Shuchi-kavaran (a medicine) is required.

Sadhu. That Atapa which the Barah Ranee sent for offerings of prayer is in the other room. Raychurn, bring that here.

(Exit Raychurn.)

Reboti. Is Annapurnah † now awake, that she shall with the rice in her hands come to me my Khetromani? It is through my ill-fate that our mistress is become mad.

Physician. She is already full of sorrow for the death of her husband ; again, her son is on the point of death ; her

---

* Thickly prepared signifies many coverings of the bed placed one above another.

† It is one of the names of Doorgah. The term signifies " full of rice," or the Goddess of Plenty.

insanity is on the increase. I think she shall die before
Nobin ; she is become very weak.

Sadhu. Sir, how did you find our eldest Babu, to-day ?
I think, with his pure blood he has extinguished the fire of
tyranny of the giants, the Indigo Planters. It is probable,
that the Indigo Commission might produce to the ryots
some advantages ; but what effect has that ? If one hundred
serpents do bite at once my whole body I can bear that ;
if on a hearth made of bricks, a frypan be placed full of
molasses, and the same be boiling by a great fire, I can also
ber the torments, if by accident I fall into the pan ; if in the
dark night of the new-moon a band of robbers with terrible
sounds come upon and kill my only son who is honest and
very learned, take away all the acquisitions made during the
past seven generations, and then make me blind: all these
also, I can bear ; and in the place of one, even if there be
ten Indigo Factories in the village, that also I can allow ;
but to be separated even for a moment from that elder Babu
who is so much the supporter of his dependants, that can I
never bear.

Physician. The blow through which the brain has oozed
out is fatal. I have found the pulse indicate that death is
near ; either at mid-day or in the evening, life will depart.
Bipin gave a little water of the Ganges in his mouth, but it
came out by its sides. Nobin's wife is quite distracted ; but
she is trying her utmost for his safety.

Sadhu. Ah! Ah! Had our mistress not been insane, her
heart would have been burst asunder on seeing this. The
doctor has also said, that the bruise on the head is fatal.

Physician. The doctor is a very kind-hearted man : when
Babu Bindu wanted to give him money, he said, " Babu
Bindu, the manner in which you are already troubled makes
it improbable that the ceremony of your father will be performed. I cannot take any thing from you now, and also it

is not necessary for you to give money for the bearers who brought me and who will now take me away." Had the doctor been of a hard heart, he would have taken away the money kept for the ceremony. I have seen that kind of doctors twice; he is as scurrilous as avaricious.

Sadhu. Our young Babu brought along with him the doctor to see Khetromani; but he said nothing with certainty. The doctor observing my want, owing to the tyranny of the Planters, gave, me two rupees in the name of Khetromani.

Physician. Had the doctor been hard-hearted he would have taken hold of the hand, and said, she would die; and he would have taken the money by selling your kine.

Reboti. I can give money by selling off whatever I have, if they can only cure my Khetro.

Enter RAYCHURN *with the rice.*

Physician. Having washed the rice, bring the water here. (*Reboti takes the rice*). Do not give much water. I see the plate is very beautiful.

Reboti. Our mistress (Sabitri) went to Gya and brought many plates; and she gave this to my Khetro. Ah! the same mistress is now turned mad, and her hands are bound with a rope, because she is slapping her cheeks.

Physician. Sadhu, bring the stone-mortar, I have the medicine here. (*Opens his box of medicine.*)

Sadhu. Sir, don't bring out your medicine; just see, how her eyes appear. Raychurn, come here.

Reboti. Oh mother! What is my fate now! Oh mother, how shall I forget the figure of Harana! Oh! Oh! Oh Khetro, Oh Khetro! Khetromoni! daughter. Wilt thou not speak any more, my daughter? Oh! Oh! Oh! (*Weeps*).

Physician. Her end is very near.

Sadhu Raychurn take hold of her, take hold of her (*Sadhuchurn and Raychurn take Khetramoni from the. bed, and go out-side*).

Reboti. I cannot leave my Laksmi of gold to float on the water. Where shall I go? Had she lived with the Saheb, that would have been better. I would have remained at rest by seeing her face. My daughter, ho! ho! ho! *(Goes behind Khetra, slapping herself).*

Physician. I die! I die! I die! What pains does the mother bear! It is good not to have a child.

(Exit all.)

FIFTH ACT—FOURTH SCENE.

The Hall in the House of Goluk Chunder Basu.

Sabitri sitting with the dead body of Nobin on her lap.

Sabitri. Let my dear child sleep; my dear keeps my heart at rest. When I see the sweet face, I remember that other face* *(kisses).* My child is sleeping most soundly *(rubs the hand over the head of the corpse).* Ah! what have the mus-quitoes done? What shall I do for the heat? I must not lie down without letting the curtains fall *(rubs the hand on the breast of the body)* Ah! Can the mother suffer this, to see the bugs bite the child and let drops of blood come out. No one is here to prepare the bed of the child; how shall I let it lie down. I have no one for me; but all are gone with my husband. *(Weeps).* Oh unfortunate creature that I am! I am crying with my child here *(observing the face of Nobin).* The child of the sorrowful woman is now making *deulu†* *(kissing the mouth).* No, my dear, I have forgotten

---

* The face of her husband.

† It sometimes happens, that during sleep the child either cries or laughs; that is called, the Deala of the child.

all distress in seeing thee ; I am not weeping (*placing the pap on its mouth*) ; my dear, suckle the pap, my dear, suckle it ; I entreated the bad woman so much, even fell at her feet, still she did not bring my husband for once ; he would have gone after settling about the milk of the child. This stupid person has such a friendship with Yama, that if she had written a letter, he would have immediately given him leave (*seeing the rope in her hand*). The husband never gets salvation if on his death the widow still wears ornaments ; although I wept with such loud cries, still they made me wear the shanka.* I have burnt it by the lamp, still it is in my hands (*cuts off the rope with her teeth*). For a widow to wear ornaments it does not look good and is not tolerable. On my hands there has arisen a blister (*cries*). Whoever has stopped my wearing the shanka, let her shanka be taken off within three days† (*snaps the joints of her fingers on the ground*). Let me prepare the bed myself (*prepares the bed in fancy.*) The mat was not washed (*extends her hands a little*). I can't reach to the pillow; the coat of shreds is become dirty, (*rubs the floor with her hands*). Let me make the child lie down (*placing the dead body slowly on the ground.*) My son, what fear near a mother ? You lie down peacefully. I shall spit here (*spits on its breast*). If that Englishman's lady come here this day, I shall kill her by pressing down her neck. I shall never have my child out of my sight. Let me place the bow round it (*gives a mark with her finger round the floor, while reading a certain verse as a sacred formula read to a God*). "The froth of the serpent, the tiger's nose, the fire prepared by the Sala's‡ resin, the whistling of the

---

* An ornament made of shell for the wrists of women.

† That is, let her become a widow within three days, who has made me so.

‡ The Sala is the native name of the tree *Shorea robusta*.

swinging machine, the white hairs of seven co-wives*—
bhanti † leaves, the flowers of the *dhuturá*, the seeds of the
Indigo, the burnt pepper, the head of the corpse, the root of
the *maddar*, the mad dog, the thief's reading of the Chundi ;
these together make the arrow to be directed against the
gnashing teeth of Yama."

Enter SARALOTA.

Saralota. Where are these gone to ? Ah ! she is turning
round the dead body. I think, my husband, tired with
excessive travelling, has given himself up to Sleep, that
goddess who is the destroyer of all sorrows and pains. Oh
Sleep ! how very miraculous is thy greatness, thou makest
the widow to be with her husband in this world, thou bringest
the traveller to his country ; at thy touch, the prisoner's
chain breaks ; thou art the Dhannantari ‡ of the sick ; thou
hast no distinction of castes in thy dominions ; and thy laws
are never different on account of the difference of nations or
castes ; thou must have made my husband a subject of thy
impartial power ; or else, how is it, that the insane mother
brings away the dead son from him. My husband is become
quite distracted by being deprived of his father and his brother. The beauty of his countenance has faded by and by,
as the full-moon decreases day by day. My mother, when
hast thou come up ? I have left off food and sleep, and am
looking after thee continually ; and did I fall into so much
insensibility ; I promised, that I shall bring thy husband from
Yama, (Invisible) in order to cure thee, and therefore thou
remainedest quiet for sometime. In this formidable night, so
full of darkness, like unto that which shall take place on the
destruction of the Universe ; when the skies are spread over
with the terrors of the clouds, the flashes of lightning are

---

* The wives of the same husband.

† *Volkmeria odorata.*

‡ Dhannantari is the Physician of the Gods.

giving a momentary light, like the arrows of fire, and the race of living creatures are given up, as it were, to the sleep of Death; all are silent; when the only sound is the cry of jackals in the wilderness and the loud noise of the dogs, the great band of enemies to thieves. My mother, how is it possible, that in such a night as this thou wast able to bring thy dead son from out-side the house. (*Goes near the corpse*).

Sabitri. I have placed the circle; and why do you come within it?

Saralota. Ah! my husband can never be able to live on seeing the death of this his land-conquering and most dear brother. (*Weeps*).

Sabitri. You are envying my child; you all-destroying wretch, the daughter of a wretch! Let your husband die. Go out, just now; be out; or else, I shall place my foot on your throat, take out your tongue and kill you immediately.

Saralota. Ah! such Shoranan* (six-mouthed) of gold, whom our father-in-law and mother-in-law had, is now gone into the water.

Sabitri. Don't look on my child; I forbid you—you destroyer of your husband. I see, your death is very near. (*Goes a little towards her*).

Saralota. Ah! how very cruel are the formidable arms of Death? Ah Yama! you gave so much pain to my honest mother-in-law.

Sabitri. Calling again! Calling again! (*takes hold of Saralota's neck by her two hands and throws her down on the ground*). Thou stupid, beloved of Yama. Now will I kill thee (*stands upon her neck*). Thou hast devoured my

---

* Shoranan is one of the names of Kartikeya. In this place, it refers to Nobin Madhab, on account of the great honor which he had acquired from the people of the country; and he is compared with Kartikeya, because he had much honour among the gods.

husband ; again, thou art calling your paramour to swallow my dear infant. Die, die, die, die now. (*Begins to skip upon the neck.*)

Saralota. Gah, a, a, (*death of Saralota.*)

Enter BINDU MADHAB.

Bindu. Oh ! She is lying flat here. Oh mother, what is that ? Thou hast killed my Saralota (*taking hold of Saralota's head*). My dear Sarala has left this sinful world. (*After weeping, kisses Saralota.*)

Sabitri. Gnaw the wretch and destroy her. She was calling Yama to devour my infant ; and therefore I killed her. (*Standing on her neck*).

Bindu. As the mother, having destroyed the child whom she was fondling for making it sleep on her lap, on awaking will go to destroy herself, so wilt thou, Oh my mother ! go to kill thyself, if thine insanity passing off thou can'st understand, that thy most beloved Saralota was murdered by thee. It will be good if that lamp no more give its light to thee. Ah ! how very pleasant it is for a woman to be mad, who has lost her husband and son ! The deer-like mind being enclosed within the stone walls of madness can never be attacked by the great tiger Sorrow. I am thy Bindu Madhab.

Sabitri. What, what do you say ?

Bindu. Mother, I can no longer keep my life, becoming mad by the death of my father bound by the rope, and the death of my elder brother ; thou hast destroyed my Saralota, and thus hast applied salt to my wounded heart.

Sabitri. What ! Is my Nobin dead ! Is my Nobin dead ! Ah, my dear son, my dear Bindu Madhab ! Have I killed your Saralota ? Have I killed my young Bou by becoming mad (*embracing the dead body of Saralota*). I would have remained alive, although deprived of my husband and my son.

Ah, but on murdering you by my own hands, my heart is on the point of being burnt. Ho! Ho! Mother, (*embracing Saralota, she falls down dead on the ground*).

Bindu. (*Placing his hand on Sabitri's body.*) What I said, took place actually. My mother died on recovering her understanding. What affliction! My mother will no more take me on her lap, and kiss me. Oh mother! the word mama will no more come out of my mouth, (*weeps*). Let me place the dust of her feet on my head (*takes the dust from her feet and places that on his own head*). Let me also purify my body by eating that dust. (*Eats the dust of her feet*).

Enter SOIRINDRI.

Soirindri. I am going to die with my husband; do not oppose me, my brother-in-law? My Bipin shall live happily with Saralota. What's this, what's this? Why are our mother-in-law and bou both lying in this manner?

Bindu. Oh eldest Bou! our mother first killed Saralota, then getting her understanding again, she fell into such excess of sorrow, that she also died.

Soirindri. Now! In what manner? What loss! What is this! What is this! Ah! Ah! my sister, thou hast not yet worn that most pleasant lock of hair on the head which. I prepared for thee! Ah! ah! thou shalt no more call me, sister (*cries*). Mother-in-law, thou art gone to your Rama, but did'st not let me go there. Oh my mother-in-law, when I got thee, I did not for a moment remember my mother.

Enter ADURI.

Aduri. Oh eldest Haldarni, come soon; thy young Bipin is afraid.

Soirindri. Why did you not call me thence? You left him there alone. (*Goes out hastily with Aduri*).

Bindu. My Bipin is now the pole-star in the ocean of dangers ! *(with a deep sigh).* In this world of short existence, human life is as the bank of a river which has a most violent course and the greatest depth. How very beautiful are the banks, the fields covered over with new grass, most pleasant to the view, the trees full of branches newly coming out ; in some places the cottages of fishermen ; in others the kine feeding with their young ones. To walk about in such a place enjoying the sweet songs of the beautiful birds, and the charming gale full of the sweet smell of flowers, only wraps the mind in the contemplation of that Being who is full of pleasure. Accidentally, a hole small as a line is observed in the field, and immediately that most pleasant bank falls down into the stream. How very sorrowful ! The Bose family of Svaropur is destroyed by Indigo, the great destroyer of honour. How very terrible are the arms of Indigo !

The cobra de capello, like the Indigo Planters, with mouths full of poison, threw all happiness into the flame of fire. The father, through injustice, died in the prison ; the elder brother in the Indigo-field, and the mother, being insane through grief for her husband and son, murdered with her own hands a most honest woman. Getting her understanding again, and observing my sorrow, the ocean of grief again swelled in her. With that disease of sorrow came the poison of want ; and thus without attending to consolation, she also departed this life. Incessantly do I call, Where is my father ? Where is my father ? Embrace me once more with a smiling face. Crying out, Oh mother ! Oh mother ! I look on all sides ; but that countenance of joy do I find no where. When I used to call, Mama, she immediately took me on her breast, and rubbed my mouth. Who knows the greatness of maternal affection ? The cry of mama, mama, mama, mama do I make in the battle-field and the wilderness whenever fear arises in the mind. Oh my brother, dear unto the heart, in the place of whom there is not one, as a friend in this world ! Thy Bindu Madhab is come ! open thine eyes once more and see. Ah ! ah ! it bursts my heart, not to know where my heart's Sarala is gone to. The most beautiful, wise, and entirely devoted to me ; she walked as the swan,* and her eyes were handsome as those of the deer. With a smiling face and with the sweetest voice, thou didst read to me the *Betal*. The mind was charmed by thy sweet reading which was as the singing of the bird in the forest. Thou, Sarala, hadst a most beauteous face, and didst brighten the lake of my heart. Who did take away my lotus with a cruel heart ? The beautiful lake became dark. The world I look upon is as a desert full of corpses ; while I have lost my father, my mother, my brother, and my wife.

Ah ! where are they gone to in search of the dead body of my brother ? I am to prepare for going to the Ganges as soon as they come. Ah ! how very terrible, the last scene of the drama of the lion-like Nobin Madhab is ? (*Sits down, taking hold of Sabitri's feet*).

[*The curtain falls down.*

---

* The gait of the swan is considered in this country the most beautiful model of the motion of the feet.

FINIS.

Calcutta Printing and Publishing Press, No. 10, Weston's Lane.